Casey turned back to face him. "And what's that?"

Clint smiled. "I think you're underestimating just what you're up against . . . and overestimating yourself."

Casey stared at him. Clint wasn't standing properly. He was stiff and in pain from his healing wounds. Casey didn't think he had a choice anymore. He'd have to alter his plans later on, but right now, his primary problem was Clint Adams.

"We can go out in the street," Casey said. "If you outdraw me, you can leave this town with no problems."

"Well, that makes us even, then," Clint said.

Casey squinted. "How so?"

"If I kill you," Clint said, "all your problems will be solved . . . permanently."

DON'T MISS THESE
ALL-ACTION WESTERN SERIES
FROM THE BERKLEY PUBLISHING GROUP

THE GUNSMITH by J. R. Roberts
> Clint Adams was a legend among lawmen, outlaws, and ladies. They called him . . . the Gunsmith.

LONGARM by Tabor Evans
> The popular long-running series about U.S. Deputy Marshal Long—his life, his loves, his fight for justice.

SLOCUM by Jake Logan
> Today's longest-running action Western. John Slocum rides a deadly trail of hot blood and cold steel.

BUSHWHACKERS by B. J. Lanagan
> An action-packed series by the creators of Longarm! The rousing adventures of the most brutal gang of cutthroats ever assembled—Quantrill's Raiders.

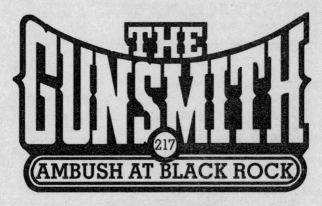

THE GUNSMITH

217

AMBUSH AT BLACK ROCK

J. R. ROBERTS

JOVE BOOKS, NEW YORK

This is a work of fiction. Names, characters, places, and incidents are either the product of the author's imagination or are used fictitiously, and any resemblance to actual persons, living or dead, business establishments, events or locales is entirely coincidental.

AMBUSH AT BLACK ROCK

A Jove Book / published by arrangement with
the author

PRINTING HISTORY
Jove edition / January 2000

The Penguin Putnam Inc. World Wide Web site address is
http://www.penguinputnam.com

ISBN: 0-515-12735-3

A JOVE BOOK®
Jove Books are published by The Berkley Publishing Group,
a division of Penguin Putnam Inc.,
375 Hudson Street, New York, New York 10014.
JOVE and the "J" design
are trademarks belonging to Penguin Putnam Inc.

PRINTED IN THE UNITED STATES OF AMERICA

10 9 8 7 6 5 4 3 2 1

THE GUNSMITH

217

AMBUSH AT BLACK ROCK

ONE

When the door was kicked in, Clint had a whiskey bottle in his left hand. The glass he was filling was sitting on a table in front of him, just to his left. Thinking back over it later, he realized how lucky he'd been all his life and wondered if he'd finally used it all up in Black Rock, New Mexico.

Of course, thinking back, he was able to reconstruct the events, but at the time everything had happened too fast for him to do anything but react.

He'd probably been lulled into a false sense of security by how sleepy the town seemed and by the fact that he'd just had sex with a beautiful woman, whose scent was still in his nostrils.

The sound of the door being kicked in startled him, and if that hadn't awakened him, the bullet that shattered the bottle in his hand did. Even as he felt the bullets tearing into him, he reacted instinctively, drawing his gun and firing blindly toward the door. He thought he caught a glimpse of four or five men, but by then they were all firing at him. More glass shattered, and he threw himself down to the floor behind an ornate red sofa. More lead smacked into the sofa, but by then it had started to get dark, and he thought he'd finally done it,

1

he'd finally taken that one misstep he'd been waiting years for and gotten himself killed. . . .

The next time he opened his eyes, the world was hazy, but still there.

"He's awake, doctor," a voice said. He couldn't tell if it was a man's or a woman's voice, because it sounded distorted to him, like it was coming from the end of a tunnel.

A face appeared above him, peering down.

"Can you hear me?" someone asked.

He opened his mouth to reply, but no sound came out. He tried to wet his lips with his tongue, but it seemed to be too heavy, to clumsy to control, and then suddenly the darkness came back again. . . .

He'd arrived in Black Rock a couple of days before the incident—what he would come to think of as his own murder. It was a small town in New Mexico, somewhere between Albuquerque and Santa Rosa. He'd ridden past Santa Rosa because it hadn't appealed to him, and he already knew he didn't want to go to Albuquerque. When he saw the sign for Black Rock, a town he had never been to before, he decided to stop.

He found friendly people, for the most part, especially the clerk at the hotel where he was staying, the bartender in the saloon he'd chosen to drink in, and even the sheriff, who didn't seem to mind having Clint Adams in his town.

"If you cause trouble," Sheriff Mike Casey said, "then I'll ask you to leave. Until then, you're one of our guests."

And, of course, there was Inga. She was blonde and had come all the way from Sweden to Black Rock to open a small apothecary shop. He saw her through the window of her shop and was compelled by her beauty to stop inside and talk to her. The attraction between them was immediate and undeniable. They were in her bed that night, and the next. On the third morning, as he was pouring himself a drink before leaving her place, the door to her shop was kicked in and he was shot to pieces and—he thought—killed. . . .

The next time he woke up things were instantly clearer than they had been before. The first thing he noticed, to his shock and delight, was that he was still alive. The next thing he noticed was that everything hurt. He couldn't even move his head.

"Hey," he said—or thought he did. Instead, it came out as an unintelligible croak. He wet his lips—his tongue worked this time—and tried it again, with more success. This time it sounded vaguely like "hey." He didn't know if anyone was around to hear it.

He had his answer in seconds. A face appeared above him, a beautiful face with shining blonde hair and liquid blue eyes.

"Clint? Can you hear me?"

"Inga?"

"Yes, it's Inga," she said in her faint swedish accent, which she had worked so hard to overcome. He had told her that he didn't see a need to overcome it, but she said that since she was living in America she wanted to sound American. He didn't think she ever would, but he kept that opinion to himself.

"Don't exert yourself," she said. "I'm going to get the doctor. Will you stay awake this time?"

"Stay awake?"

"Yes."

"Have I been awake before?"

"Several times, but never for very long."

He thought it over for a few moments, and then he told her, "All right, I'll stay awake."

"Good. I'll get the doctor and be right back."

Her face disappeared.

"Wait . . ."

She returned. "What is it?"

"What happened?"

"What do you remember?"

"I remember . . . being killed."

She smiled and said, "You were shot, but you were not killed. You are very much alive."

"Who shot me?"

"Oh my . . ."

"What?"

"Well, the sheriff was hoping you could tell us that."

He frowned, then said, "Okay, go get the doctor, but bring the sheriff, too."

"Maybe you should see the doctor first."

"I'd like to see the sheriff while I'm awake, Inga."

"All right," she said. "I will be right back."

As she left, he started to close his eyes but was afraid he'd fall back to sleep, so he forced them open again. He stared at the ceiling and tried to replay the shooting in his head, tried to figure out how many men there were and maybe put some faces to them. He found himself growing weary, but he'd promised Inga he would stay awake. He found a crack in the ceiling and started following it, moving only his eyes, first to one end of the room, and then to the other. There it even continued down the wall, but before it reached the floor he lost sight of it. He was going to have to find something else to keep him awake.

The more he thought about it the more he thought there were five men. He'd had very little contact with anyone since coming to town. Only the desk clerk, the bartender, the sheriff, and Inga. Could one of them have set him up to be killed? And why? Simply because of who he was? If that was the reason, and if the men thought they had killed him, then at some point—some-where—they were going to start bragging.

And when they did that, he'd find them.

TWO

When Inga returned, she had the doctor in tow. As promised, Clint had managed to stay awake.

"Well, well," the doctor said, "how do you feel, Mr. Adams?"

"Like I've been shot."

"You were, indeed."

The doctor was in his fifties, wearing a white shirt with his sleeves rolled up, as if Inga caught him in the middle of something. His name was Doctor Edward Milburn.

"How bad, Doc?" Clint asked.

"I'm gonna have a look right now, but I'll tell you one thing."

"What's that?"

"If ever I saw a man who had every right to be dead, it's you."

"How's that?"

"You were hit four times," the doctor said. "Once high up on the back, on the right side; once down low on the back, left side. You took a bullet in the left arm and one in the left side. Four pieces of lead that somehow avoided hitting anything vital. You lost a lot of blood, but I managed to save you."

"I guess I should be glad you're such a good doctor."

"I'm more lucky than good, Mr. Adams. Hold still a while so I can examine your wounds."

The doctor had to roll him to the right, and then to the left, to take a look.

"Does it hurt you to lie on your back?"

Clint thought a moment, then said, "Now that you mention it."

"Well, now that you're awake you can lie on your right side, if you want. That's about the only side you have available to you."

Clint rolled onto his right and found himself more comfortable.

"How long will it take me to mend?"

"Weeks," the doctor said, "and probably months before you're back to normal."

Clint frowned, not liking the sound of that. By that time the men who had shot him would be long gone, probably scattered to the four corners.

"Doc, do you know who shot me?"

"I haven't the faintest idea," the doctor said. "That's not my department. My job was to keep you alive."

"Well, thanks for doing it, lucky or not," Clint said. He looked past the doctor at Inga. "Did you talk to the sheriff?"

"Yes, he'll be along soon."

"I don't want you to move around much," the doctor said. "You'll have to stay in this bed for a while."

Clint looked around the room, recognized it as Inga's. They had spent an energetic night in this bed before he was shot.

"He can stay as long as it takes," Inga said.

"That's good," the doctor said, and then looked at her. "You gonna be nursing him?"

"Yes."

"Well, keep him still and make sure he eats. He's got

to get his strength up." He looked at Clint then. "The more you eat, the better."

"I'll remember that."

"I'll be in from time to time to check on you."

"I'll be here."

Clint put out his right hand and the doctor shook it. The man turned, nodded to Inga, and left.

"Inga?"

"Yes?"

"Where's my gun?"

"In a drawer—"

"Would you hang it on the bedpost for me, please?"

"Why do you need it?"

"I don't know if I'll need it or not," he said, "but I'd like to have it within reach."

"Clint," she said, "you're not supposed to move around."

"Inga," he said, "what happens if those men come back to finish the job? I'd be a sitting duck in this bed. Please, hang the holster on the bedpost?"

She thought a moment, then said, "Oh, all right."

She took it out of a dresser drawer and hung it on the bedpost so he could reach it with his right hand if he had to. Suddenly, there was a knock on the door.

"That would be the sheriff," she said as she answered the door. It was Sheriff Mike Casey.

"He's not supposed to exert himself," Inga warned Casey.

"He asked for me, Inga. Remember?"

"Just so you know." She looked at Clint. "I'll get you something to eat."

"Thanks." He realized that he felt hungry.

As Inga left the room, Casey approached the bed. He was a tall, rangy man made to look even taller by the fact that Clint was confined to the bed.

"Do you know what happened?" Casey asked.

"I know I was shot four times," Clint said. "Do you know who shot me, Sheriff?"

"Nope," Casey said. "I was hopin' you'd tell me that."

"I didn't see—" Clint started, then stopped as something flashed into his mind and then vanished.

"What is it?" Casey asked. "Do you need the doc?"

"No," Clint said, "no . . ."

"So you didn't see them?"

"No, I didn't. I did get off a shot, though."

"I thought you might have," Casey said. "I found some blood that was too far away from you to be yours."

"Did anyone see anything? Hear anything?"

"Not that we know of."

"Why not?"

Casey shrugged.

"It was early."

"What have you found out?"

"Nothing."

"Why not? Have you asked—"

Casey held up his hand.

"I'm a small-town sheriff, Mr. Adams," the lawman said, "not a detective. If you have any suggestions, I'm open to them."

Clint thought a moment and shifted on the bed in an attempt to get more comfortable.

"All right," he said, "they had horses, right? They would have needed them for a quick getaway."

"Right."

"Check with the livery," Clint said. "They would have to get the horses from someplace. If not the livery, is there anyone nearby who deals in horses?"

"One man, that I know of."

"Check with him, too. Find out who bought four or five horses."

"Wouldn't they already have had their own horses?"

"I'm hoping they wanted fresh ones," Clint said. "If

they each had their own already and used them, then we're out of luck."

"All right. Anything else?"

"Yes," Clint said. "Eventually they're going to brag about this; otherwise, there would have been no sense in doing it. I'll need some paper and a pencil, and you to send a telegram for me."

"Done."

THREE

The doctor returned that evening after Inga had fed Clint some soup for dinner. Once again, he examined Clint's wounds.

"Did you talk to the sheriff?" he asked.

"Yes, he stopped by not long after you did."

"Did you resolve anything?"

"Such as?"

"Such as who shot you."

"Nobody knows," Clint said. "Apparently, there were no witnesses to the shooting, or to the shooters' escape."

"Too bad."

"Yeah, it is."

"And you still don't remember seeing anyone?"

Again there was that flash in his mind, but it quickly faded.

"No."

The doctor redressed his wounds and said, "No need to change the dressings until tomorrow. I'll be back during the day."

"Thanks, Doc."

"Thank me when you get my bill. I'll see you tomorrow."

Clint watched the doctor walk to the door but never saw him go through it. He fell asleep that quickly.

When Doctor Milburn returned to his office, two men were waiting for him. They were both in their late twenties, wearing trail-worn clothes and tied-down handguns.

"So?" one of them asked.

"So what?" Milburn put down his black bag and faced the two men.

"Did he see us?" the other man asked.

"He says he didn't see anybody," Milburn said. "Not you or any of the others."

Jed Tyler and Warren Marks exchanged a glance.

"Is he telling the truth?" Tyler asked.

"Who knows?"

"You're supposed to know," Marks said.

"I'm a doctor, not a mind reader," Milburn said. "If Cahill wants him dead, why did he make me save him?"

"He wants to do it himself," Tyler said.

"Five of you?" Milburn asked. "That's what he calls doing it himself?"

"He was there," Tyler said.

"He pulled the trigger," Marks added, "just like the rest of us."

At that point there was a knock on the door. Milburn went and opened it, admitting Sheriff Mike Casey.

"What are you doing here?" he demanded of the two men.

"Cahill sent us," Tyler answered.

"Where is he?"

"Far away."

"He better be. Are the other two with him?"

"Yes," Marks said.

"Well, you boys better join him. I want you far away from here."

"Hey, wait—" Marks started, but Casey cut him off.

"No, you wait," the lawman said. "You men had a job to do, and you botched it."

"We hit him!" Tyler said.

"Four times," Milburn said. "He's a hard man to kill."

"And now we have to wait for him to mend before we try again," Casey said. "Meantime, I don't want any of you coming back to town."

"Doc says Adams didn't see any of us," Tyler said.

"I'm not going to take any chances," Casey said. "Stay away from here until I send for you. Tell Cahill."

"We'll tell him," Marks said, "but he ain't gonna like it."

"I don't care whether he likes it or not," Sheriff Casey said. "Now get going."

"It's dark," Marks said.

"You won't get lost."

Again, the two men exchanged a glance, and then started for the door.

"Use the back door, for Chrissake!" Casey snapped.

Both men looked chastened but said nothing. They turned and went out the back door.

"Morons," Casey said. "Why'd you let them in here?"

"They were here when I got back."

"How's Adams?"

"He's gonna make it."

Casey ran his hand over his face.

"He says he may want us to say that he died."

"That's a good idea, from his point of view," Milburn said. "Have you told—"

"No," Casey said, "I haven't seen him, yet."

"When will you?"

"Tomorrow morning," Casey said. "I'll ride out there to see him tomorrow morning."

"How do you think he's gonna take it?"

"How does he take it when anything doesn't go right?" Sheriff Casey asked.

"Will we lose our jobs?"

"No."

"Why not?"

"Because he doesn't have anyone who can do them better right now," Casey explained.

"I hope you're right."

"I'm right," Casey said. "Adams gave me a telegram to send."

"To who?"

"Some fella in Labyrinth, Texas."

"What's it about?"

"He expects the shooters to start braggin' pretty soon," Casey said. "This fella is supposed to locate them."

"So don't send it."

"I've got to send it," Casey said. "Adams will know something's wrong if I don't. What we need is for Cahill and the others to keep their mouths shut. If they don't start braggin', then they won't be easy to locate."

"And what are the chances that they won't brag?"

"That bunch?" Casey asked. "Not much."

"So when Adams gets on his feet he'll go after them."

"Right."

"And when he catches them he catches us."

"Wrong," Casey said. "I'm not goin' down with those morons, and neither are you."

"How do you figure?"

"Because they'll be too dead to give us up."

"You think Adams can kill all five?"

"Sure, why not?" Casey said.

"Five against one?"

"It was five against one before, wasn't it? And they still had to ambush him. Besides, he can take them out one at a time."

"And what if he doesn't?"

"That's easy," Sheriff Mike Casey said, "because if he doesn't kill them, I will."

FOUR

As Inga entered the room, Clint came awake. This was a good sign, because she had made hardly any sound at all when entering.

"I'm sorry I woke you," she said.

"That's okay," Clint said. "At least I'm alert."

She came to the bed, pulled over a chair, and sat by him.

"Do you think those men will come back?"

"Probably not. I'm sorry if there was damage downstairs, to your shop, I mean."

"Damage to the shop?" she repeated. "That doesn't matter, Clint. My God, when I came down and saw you lying there all covered with blood, I thought you were dead. I didn't care about the damage."

"I appreciate that, but . . ."

"But what?"

"I've been lying here wondering."

"Wondering what?"

"Why they chose your place to ambush me," he said. "How they knew I'd be there at that time of the morning."

"I think people . . . knew about us," she said.

17

"But how did they know I'd be in the shop and not up here with you?" he asked.

"I don't know."

"Somebody must have been watching, waiting for me to come down," he reasoned. "Somebody must have been outside your shop, waiting."

"Who?"

"Nobody knows," he said. "At least, nobody is saying." He shifted in bed, tried to settle onto his back, but it was too uncomfortable.

"Here," Inga said, standing up. She took one of his two pillows and laced it carefully behind him, between his wounds. He was able to lie back without compressing his injuries.

"Thanks."

She smiled and sat back down.

"I can't believe that no one saw a man loitering out front. No one saw four or five men on horseback. No one heard the shots."

"I heard them," she said, "and the sheriff heard them, because he was the first one to arrive, after me."

"Don't people in this town stir early?"

"There are usually people on the street when I open," she said, "but I open at ten."

"This bothers me."

"What do you think it means?"

He frowned and said, "I'm not sure. I'm still thinking about it."

"Do you want anything before I go to bed?"

He reached out and took her hand.

"You've been wonderful to me. I'd probably be dead if it wasn't for you."

"The doctor saved you."

"Where are you sleeping? I mean, since I've got your bed."

"I have a guest room down the hall," she said. "The bed there is quite comfortable."

"I hate putting you out."

"You're not." She stood up. "Can I get you something?"

"No, I'm fine."

She leaned over the bed and kissed him gently on the mouth.

"That was nice," he said. "Some more of that would be very nice."

"The doctor said you are not to exert yourself," she said, straightening. "You will get more of that when you feel better."

"That's just what I needed," he said. "Incentive to get better."

"Good night, Clint."

"Good night, Inga."

After Inga left, Clint reached up for his gun and slid it out of the holster. He checked to make sure it was loaded and then returned it to its place. The move reaching for the gun caused him some pain, but the alternative—not reaching for the gun and possibly getting killed—was not acceptable.

He was still bothered that there were no witnesses to anything that had happened before or after the shooting. It just didn't seem possible to him. He was also wondering when his reply from Rick Hartman would come. As long as he knew he had Rick on the lookout for the men who shot him, he wouldn't feel such a sense of urgency to get on their trail. He wanted to make sure that he healed properly, that he'd be completely recovered when he got on their trail.

Suddenly, he thought of Duke in the livery stable. If they'd shot him in an ambush, had they tried anything with Duke? He decided to ask Inga to check on the big black gelding in the morning. He'd feel better knowing that the horse was safe.

There were more things going through his mind, but at that moment it chose to shut down on him, and he fell asleep.

FIVE

True to his word, the doctor stopped by the next morning to check on Clint. Inga brought coffee for both men while Milburn changed the dressings on Clint's wounds.

"May I watch?" Inga asked.

"It won't be pretty," the doctor warned her.

"If I watch," she said, "then I will be able to do it myself."

Milburn looked at her over his shoulder for a moment and then said, "Good girl."

After the wounds were cleaned and the dressings changed, the doctor asked Inga, "Think you can do that?"

"I know I can."

"Good," Milburn said, standing up from the chair he'd been sitting in to take care of his business, "because I've got other patients—not that you're not the most important one, Mr. Adams."

"I don't need to be the most important, Doc."

"Well, you are," Milburn said. "I fought tooth and nail to pull you through, and I intend to see that you stay healthy."

"Well," Clint said, "when you put it like that."

21

"I'll try to stop by tonight," Milburn said. "Take care—both of you."

"We will," Inga said.

"Doc, is the sheriff around today?"

Milburn stopped short. He happened to know that the sheriff left town early that morning, but he didn't say that. Instead, he said, "I haven't seen him, but if I do can I give him a message?"

"Just wondering about a telegram I had him send for me."

"He told me about that," Milburn said. "He told the clerk to bring it to me if he wasn't around. The minute it gets here, I'll see that you get it."

"I'd be much obliged, Doc."

Milburn nodded and left the room.

"Inga, I wonder if you would do me a favor today?"

"Anything."

"Will you check on my horse at the livery? I want to make sure he's okay."

"I don't know very much about horses."

"Just check that he's still there, and then tell the liveryman to take care of him."

"All right," she said. "I'll take care of it now."

"Thank you."

"You stay still while I'm gone."

"As still as the dead."

Before leaving the room she said, "That's not funny."

Sheriff Mike Casey drove out to the Double D ranch to see the man who had given him his job. One of the ranch hands took his horse as he mounted the steps to the two-story house and knocked on the door. A black man answered it and showed no surprise at having a lawman at the door.

"Good morning, Sheriff."

"Good morning, Cyrus," Casey said. "Can I see him?"

"Of course," the man said. "He is having breakfast. I will take you back."

Casey stepped into the house, waited for Cyrus to close the door, then followed him through the huge entry foyer into the dining room.

Brian Bennett sat at a dining room table large enough for a dozen people. He was eating breakfast alone, as he did every morning. His wife, Gloria, did not usually rise for at least another two or three hours, depending on how drunk she was when she went to bed.

"The sheriff is here to see you, sir," Cyrus said.

Bennett smiled at the lawman.

"Come in, Mike," he said. "Pull up a chair. Have you had breakfast yet?"

"No, sir. Haven't had time to eat."

"Cyrus, tell the cook to prepare a plate for the sheriff. Steak and eggs all right, Mike?"

"Uh, yeah, that's fine, sir."

"Come on, have a seat. I'll pour you some coffee."

Mike Casey was constantly amazed that a man his own age—late thirties—had amassed the amount of money that Brian Bennett had. He both respected and hated Bennett for it. The man lived better than he did, commanded respect because of his wealth, and frequently traveled to other cities in the country and the world. About the only thing Mike Casey had over Bennett was that he was better looking. In truth, Bennett most resembled a gnome. Casey had often wondered how he had gotten a beautiful woman like Gloria to marry him in the first place—but the obvious answer to that was money.

And Mike Casey had recently learned a lot more about Gloria Bennett than he previously knew.

Bennett poured his coffee cup full and then returned to his meal.

"What brings you out here, Sheriff?"

"It's, uh, Clint Adams, Mr. Bennett."

"What about him?" Bennett asked, popping a piece of steak into his mouth. "Has he died?"

"No, and he's not going to."

Bennett frowned.

"That wasn't part of the plan, Sheriff."

"I know."

"Where are the men who shot him?"

"Out of town."

"That's good." He picked up his coffee cup and took a swallow. "How long will it take him to recover?"

"The doctor says weeks, at least—probably longer before he can ride a horse."

"And at that time," Bennett said, putting his cup down, "he'll go looking for those men."

"Yes, sir."

"So something has to be done about them before then."

"Yes, sir."

"You'll take care of that for me, Mike?"

"I will, sir. That's what you pay me for."

"Yes, it is. Now, what about Cahill? Will there be any problem with him?"

"No, sir," Casey said, "I can deal with him."

"Let's think about this for a minute," Bennett said, gesturing with his steak knife. "The other four are of no concern to me. Deal with them any way you see fit. Cahill, though, well . . . I've used him in the past."

"I know you have."

"He's been of value to me," Bennett continued. "I like people who have been of value to me to know they can count on me. You know that as well as anyone, Mike."

"Yes, sir, I do."

Bennett thought a moment, chewing on another bite of steak thoughtfully. He ate steak for breakfast, steak for lunch, and then had a huge steak for dinner. A meal was not complete to him without beef.

"I'll want to talk to Cahill, Mike," he said, finally. "Will you arrange that for me?"

"Yes, sir, I will."

"And keep me updated on Clint Adams's condition."

"I will."

"Finish your coffee, Mike, and then you can go."

Casey did as he was told and did not say anything about the breakfast he'd been offered. In truth, he doubted the cook was even preparing one. In the months he had been working for Brian Bennett, he had never taken a meal with the man.

"I'll be on my way," he said.

"Good," Bennett said. "Thanks for coming out, Mike."

"Yes, sir."

As if he had any choice.

Cyrus appeared as if by some signal and walked him out to the foyer. When they got there they both stopped as Gloria Bennett came down the steps. Her beauty took away the breath of both men, but Cyrus looked away, as he was employed in the house as a servant.

Mike was employed by Bennett, as well, but he did not avert his eyes. She had long, chestnut-colored hair and was dressed for riding. She was tall—several inches taller than her husband, who was barely five-and-a-half feet tall—made to look even taller by the pants and boots she was wearing. Her breasts strained at the fabric of her shirt, and he knew very well what the weight of them felt like in his hands.

"Well, hello, Mike," she greeted him, as if she hadn't seen him in days, instead of only that previous night.

"Mrs. Bennett."

"Cyrus, is my husband at breakfast?"

"He is, Ma'am."

"Good, then I'll join him. Nice to see you, Mike."

"You, too, Ma'am."

He watched her walk into the dining room, then

turned to look at Cyrus, who was already holding the
door open for him.

"Quite a woman, eh, Cyrus?"

"Good day, Sheriff."

The two men locked eyes, but there was nothing read-
able in the older black man's. If he knew anything about
Casey and Gloria, he didn't show it.

"Good day, Cyrus," Casey said, and left.

SIX

Over the course of the next week or so, Clint began to sleep less and become more alert. He was able to eat more solid foods and even sit up in bed with the help of Inga.

The doctor came by less frequently and the sheriff stopped coming by, so the only person he was really seeing and talking to was Inga.

The last time Sheriff Mike Casey had visited was six days before, when the reply to Clint's telegraph message came in.

"Got your answer from your friend," Casey said as he entered the room.

"Did you read it?" Clint asked as the man handed it over.

Casey had the good sense to look embarrassed and said, "Well, yeah, I did. I kind of felt like it was my job."

Clint didn't argue. Besides, all it said was that no one had yet started bragging about shooting him and that Rick Hartman would keep his ears open and let him know as soon as he heard something.

"Who's this Hartman?" Casey asked.

"Just a friend of mine. Thanks for bringing it over, Sheriff."

"Sure," Casey said, and left.

That was six days ago.

Clint had not heard whether or not his suggestion to Casey had panned out. He didn't even know if the man had taken his suggestion about finding out where the shooters got their horses. Apparently, the man had been serious about not being a detective and wasn't taking any steps to find them. That was okay with Clint, because once he was back on his feet—and back on a horse—he was going to find them himself.

He'd awakened a couple of days earlier to a revelation. He'd had a dream about the day of the shooting. In the dream he was pouring himself a drink and standing in front of a mirror. When the shooting started he'd drawn his gun, fired one shot, and hit the floor, but even before that he looked in the mirror and caught a look at the men who had kicked in the door.

When he woke up he realized that this was more than a dream, it was what had actually happened. He'd had flashes of it for a while, but it had only become clear to him in the dream.

Now, while awake, he was able to go over the incident in his mind. In the mirror he had seen two men coming through the open door, side by side, with other men behind them. There was no way he could identify the hidden men, but the faces of the first two seemed to have crystalized in his mind. He felt sure that when he saw them again he'd be able to recognize them.

For this reason he felt no great urgency to force his recovery, or test it by getting out of bed early. He knew what two of the men looked like, and they were out there. There was no need to push himself and do more harm than good.

He had also spent a lot of time thinking about the way

he'd been caught flat-footed. For years he'd been determined not to come to the same end as his friend Jim Hickok, shot in the back by a coward. Suddenly, he'd let his guard down and had almost been killed by five cowards. That made him five times the fool Hickok had been, only he had been given a second chance, an opportunity to redeem himself, and he intended to take full advantage of that.

There was something else on his mind. He'd come to the decision that this attempt on his life could not have been pulled off without some help. Five men congregating in front of an apothecary would not go unnoticed in any town, especially not by the town lawman. To him that indicated that Sheriff Casey might have been in on it. Although he might not have been one of the men who fired the shots, he could have been paid to look the other way. That would also explain why he wasn't making any great attempts to look into the incident.

He had not told Inga of his suspicions, because the plot—if indeed there was one—could go further than the sheriff. He also didn't want to sound too paranoid.

But there was another reason. He had decided to suspect everyone. The sheriff, the doctor, even Inga. Even though her place had gotten shot up, she suggested that they spend the night in her room, and not in his hotel room.

He gave her the benefit of the doubt and suspected her the least, but he still suspected her.

Later that day Inga came in with his lunch, and he asked her to stay and talk while he ate.

"Do you want me to feed you?" she asked.

"I think we're past that," Clint said. "Look, I can even sit up myself."

He pushed himself to a seated position. She gave him a little mock applause and then fluffed his pillows behind him so he'd be comfortable. He'd been lucky enough that none of his wounds were very dangerous on their own. It had been the combination of them—and the blood loss—that had been life threatening. Now his wounds itched because they were healing, but he was surprised to find that he wasn't experiencing any real pain from any of them.

"What do you want to talk about?" she asked. She seated herself next to the bed after laying the tray of food across his lap.

"I'm trying to figure something out."

"What?"

"Who hired those men to kill me."

"What makes you think they were hired?"

"Hired, or sent," Clint said, "but I don't think they tried this on their own."

"Why not?"

"I think if they had they would have come back. I'm a pretty easy target. All they'd have to do is kick open this door like they did the one downstairs, and I'd be a sitting duck. I might get one or two of them, but they'd probably succeed just by sheer numbers."

"What makes you think I could guess who hired them?"

"You live in this town," he said, hoping she wouldn't figure out that she was a suspect and get upset with him. "You know the people here."

"Couldn't it have been someone from out of town who hired them?" she asked.

"Definitely," he said, "but you could only help me with the people in and around town. I'll have to work on the out of town part myself."

"Well, all right . . . let me think."

"Let me see if I can help you," Clint said. "It would have to be someone with enough money to pay five men to risk their lives."

"Well," she said, "I think you have made that question a very easy one. There is only one man who lives around here who would have enough money to do that."

"And who would that be?"

"Brian Bennett."

"I don't know the name."

"He moved here over a year ago and is very wealthy. He has a ranch outside of town and employs many people."

"Hmm. Do you know him well?"

"Not well, but I do know him."

"Would he be the type to hire someone to do his killing for him?"

She started to answer, probably in the negative, but stopped and thought about it for a moment.

"I was going to say no," she said, "but I simply cannot see him killing anyone himself. So I guess the answer is yes. After all, he has enough money to hire someone for any task."

"What's he like?"

"Physically?"

"Start there."

"Well, he is not an attractive man. He is very short and, well, sort of homely."

"Is he married?"

"Oh yes, and his wife is very beautiful. She must have married him for his money."

"That's not a nice thing to say."

"Well, everyone in town says so," she said, "not just me."

"You're a beautiful woman," he said. "You mean you couldn't see yourself marrying a man like him if he didn't have money?"

"Clint, I wouldn't marry a man like him if he had *twice* as much money as he has now."

"Is he mean?"

"Not that I know of."

"Then he's nice?"

"He's always been pleasant to me."

"And how does he treat his wife?"

She hesitated, then said, "You know, I haven't seen the two of them together in a long while."

"So there may be some trouble there."

"Do you think he'd hire people to have you killed because he's not getting along with his wife?"

"Only if he thought I was sleeping with her, I guess."

"Well, you weren't, were you?"

He smiled and took her hand.

"You know who I've been with since I came to town. In fact, why don't we—"

"Oh no," she said, snatching her hand away from him, "you are not ready for that, yet."

"We could take it easy—"

"No," she said, "we could not. You forget how we fell out of bed the first time."

"No," he said, "I didn't forget. After all, we finished up on the floor, and it was very memorable."

"Are you finished with your lunch?" she asked. She seemed out of breath, and her eyes were shining. Apparently, talking about the first night they were together was having an effect on her.

He knew it was having an effect on him—and that's when he knew he was feeling better.

SEVEN

Later that evening, in spite of the feeling that there was no need to try to rush his recovery, Clint had the urge to get up. He did an examination of his wounds and didn't think that getting to his feet was going to aggravate any of them. He just wanted to feel the floor again and give his butt a rest from the bed.

He sat up and maneuvered himself to the end of the bed and let his feet dangle over. It seemed to stretch the wound on his left side, but there was not enough pain to deter him. Since his legs were fine, he didn't anticipate a problem in standing up. When he did, though, he immediately became dizzy and sat back down.

He waited a few moments for the dizziness to pass, then decided to try again. He'd only gotten dizzy because he had been on his back for so long. This time he took it more slowly. He felt the wood floors beneath his bare feet, waited a moment, and then stood up carefully. The dizziness did not return. He straightened up and liked the way it felt to be standing again. He wondered if he should try to walk.

There was a window on the other side of the bed. If he had intended to walk to it he could have stood up on that side. He decided this would be a good test, to walk around the bed to the window, which he knew looked out onto the street in front of the hotel.

He took a step, then another, then another, feeling like a child walking for the first time. The doctor had done a good job with his wounds, and Inga had apparently been doing a good job with his dressings. As far as he could tell, none of his wounds had opened.

He made his way around the bed and then headed for the window. When he finally reached it he was out of breath and braced himself with a hand on either side of it. He put his head against the glass, which felt cool. When he had his breath back he opened his eyes. The street below was bustling with people—it was afternoon, after all. This, however, reinforced his feelings about the shooting incident. Somebody must have seen something, only nobody was talking.

Could the whole town have been in on it?

Feeling he was having paranoid thoughts due to exertion, he turned and walked over to the bed, taking the short way to this side of it rather than walking around it again. When he was back in bed he decided to keep his "walk" a secret, but to try to do it every day. He suddenly felt the need to have his condition improve quickly, and more quickly than the others—the doctor, the sheriff, even Inga—might think.

It was time for him to take back control.

EIGHT

What Clint didn't know about Sheriff Mike Casey was that the man hadn't been to see him in a week because he'd been away all that time, leaving a deputy named Weaver in charge.

Mike Casey had ridden out to do what Brian Bennett had told him to do, but the night before he left he met once again with Gloria Bennett. She came to the house he had at the end of town, which had come with the job. Without realizing it, Brian Bennett had given the lawman the perfect place to meet with his own wife.

"Why is he sending you away?" she asked.

"He's not sending me away," Casey said. "He's just sending me to do a job."

"You're the sheriff," she said. "Have somebody else do it."

"I'm the sheriff because he pays me," Casey said. "Besides, nobody else can do this job."

"Oh, we're sounding full of ourselves," she said.

They were lying in his bed, pressed tightly together, sticking slightly because of the sweat they'd worked up making love. She dragged her nails across his bare chest.

"How long will you be gone?"

"About a week."

"With you away," she said, "I'll have to go back to drinking again."

They had met when she and Bennett first moved to town, and Bennett hired him to be sheriff, but nothing had happened between them until he found her on the street one night, drunk. Not wanting anyone to see her that way, he took her home with him. Nothing happened that night, but she appreciated his kindness. They talked more when they saw each other after that, and eventually they became closer and closer. Finally, when they started sleeping together, she stopped drinking—although she didn't let her husband know that. Whenever she was out with Casey, he still thought she was out drinking. He didn't mind that, but if he knew she was seeing another man, he would kill her. And he would have Casey killed.

She rolled over and slid on top of him, smothering him with her full breasts. He took them in his hands and guided them to his mouth, sucking first one and then the other. After that they became a frenzy of movement, and a memory he carried with him on the trail.

Now he was outside the town of Montoya Wells, where he knew Ed Cahill was holed up. With him would be both Tyler and Marks. The other two—Simms and Jacks—were no longer a concern.

He pushed Gloria Bennett from his mind, because any distraction over the course of the next hour or so could cost him his life. When thoughts of her were in a safe place, he kicked his horse into a canter and rode toward town.

Tyler was standing at the door of the saloon when he saw Casey ride into town.

"He just rode in," he said over his shoulder.

Cahill looked up from the table he was sitting at, contemplating a beer mug, while Marks looked over from the bar.

"Want us to take him with you?" he asked Cahill.

"Just relax," Cahill said, "let's see what he wants."

"You know what he wants," Marks said. "Same thing he wanted with Simms and Jacks."

"Simms and Jacks are dead," Tyler said, still from the door.

"That's my point," Marks said.

"Settle down," Cahill said. "Tyler, go out and get him."

"Sure."

Tyler stepped outside, right to the end of the board-walk so Casey could see him. When he did, he came riding up, and Tyler noticed that the lawman wasn't wearing his badge.

Bad sign.

"Hello, Tyler," Casey said.

"Cahill's inside. He says for you to come in."

"That's what I intended to do."

Casey dismounted and went into the saloon ahead of Tyler. When he saw Cahill, he stopped. The man looked the same as ever, compact, fortyish, with long, stringy hair and maybe more beard stubble than usual.

"Mike," Cahill said. "Sit down and have a drink."

"Tell Tyler to go to the bar," Casey said. "I don't want him behind me."

"Tyler," Cahill said, "do it."

Casey looked over at the bar and said, "Marks."

Marks just nodded.

"Sit down, Mike," Cahill said. "Marks, bring the sheriff a beer."

"Sure, Cahill."

Casey walked to the table and sat adjacent to Cahill rather than across from him. He wanted to see the whole room. He waited until Marks came over with the beer and then returned to the bar to stand next to Tyler.

"You did some job on Simms and Jacks," Cahill said. "Did you take them together?"

"One at a time," Casey said. "It was safer that way."

"Why'd you kill them?"

"You know why." Casey sipped his beer, careful to hold it in his left hand.

"Orders?"

Casey nodded.

"You got orders to kill me?"

"Nope."

"Why not?"

"The man wants to talk to you."

"We did what we were supposed to do," Cahill said. "Sonofabitch just wouldn't die."

"I told you," Casey said, "I'm not here to kill you. He just wants to talk to you."

"How do I know?" Cahill asked. "How I know you ain't here to try to kill me?"

Casey sipped his beer again.

"Those two," he said, jerking his head toward the bar.

"What about them?"

"He doesn't want to see them."

Tyler and Marks both stood up straight. Casey and Cahill stared at each other for a while.

"Prove it," Cahill finally said.

Casey put his beer down and stood up.

"Hey, wait—" Tyler said.

"Cahill—" Marks said.

"You boys are on your own," Cahill said, remaining in his chair.

"Damnit—" Tyler said, and both he and Marks went for their guns.

Casey drew and fired twice. His first bullet his Tyler in the gut, the second caught Marks in the chest. Neither man had cleared leather. The slid down the bar until they were sprawled on the floor.

With his gun still out, Casey looked at Cahill, then very deliberately holstered it. He sat down and picked up his beer.

"So when do we start back?" Cahill asked.

NINE

By the time Mike Casey returned to town with Ed Cahill, Clint had taken several walks around his room without anyone the wiser. Casey's first stop was Doc Milburn's office.

"How is he?" he asked, entering.

"Well, welcome back," Milburn said. "Did you get done what you set out to do?"

"I did."

"And Cahill?"

"He's back."

"Where is he?"

"My house."

"Good," Milburn said. "He'll have to stay out of sight."

"I know that," Casey said. "How's Adams?"

"Recovering slowly," Milburn said.

"Too slowly?"

"The man was shot four times, Mike."

"But could he be doing better than he lets on?"

Milburn took a moment to think about it.

"No, I don't think so," he said, finally. "A normal man would have died on the floor before you got there, Mike."

41

"So he's not a normal man," Casey said. "We knew that going in."

"You think he's faking?" Milburn asked. "Hiding the fact that he's recovering quickly? Why?"

"I don't know," Casey said. "Maybe I just think it'll be safer to think that way."

"I'm the doctor, Mike," Milburn said, "you're the lawman. Let's keep it that way."

"Fine," Casey said. "I'm going out to see Bennett."

"Good luck."

Casey went to the door.

"The other four? Tyler and them?" Milburn asked.

Over his shoulder Casey said, "They ain't comin' back."

Milburn didn't say anything, and Casey left.

From the front window of her shop, Inga saw Mike Casey ride back into town alone. She knew very well he'd been away over a week, but she didn't know where he'd been, or why. She wondered if his absence was of any importance to Clint Adams. Should she mention it to him? How much trouble would that get her into? And did she even care?

She watched as Mike Casey rode out again.

Casey stopped at his house to pick up Cahill, and then they rode out to Brian Bennett's ranch together. They were admitted to the house by Cyrus, who took them to Bennett's office.

"Ah, Cahill," Bennett said, as he and Mike Casey entered. "Nice to have you back."

Cahill's look was a wary one.

"A drink?" Bennett asked.

"Uh, no," Cahill said.

"You seem puzzled."

"I . . . thought you'd be mad at me."

"Angry? With you? What for?"

"Well . . . Adams is still alive."

"Oh, yes," Bennett said, "there is that, isn't there. Well . . ."

Without warning, Bennett took a gun from his desk top, pointed it at Cahill, and fired three times. The man went from shocked to dead after one shot. The other two were just icing.

Mike Casey jumped back as Ed Cahill slumped to the ground, his hand hovering near his gun.

"Don't," Bennett said, covering him with his weapon, which was still cocked.

"What's this about?" Casey asked. "You asked me to bring him back here so you could kill him in front of me?"

"Precisely."

"That's crazy," Casey said. "Why?"

"To prove a point."

"What point?"

"That I'm not afraid to do my own killing, Mike," Bennett said.

"That's obvious."

"Good!" Bennett said. "I wanted it to be obvious. I'm going to put my gun away now. Please don't draw yours."

"I won't."

"Cyrus?"

"Yes, sir?"

The old black man had obviously been nearby, yet he had not come running in at the sound of the shot.

"Get someone to remove this body."

"Yes, sir."

"Mike, come with me," Bennett said. "We'll talk in the den."

They left the office with the shorter man leading. When they reached the den, Bennett poured them each a glass of brandy.

"Here," he said, handing Casey his. "It'll settle your nerves."

"I don't have any nerves."

"Drink it anyway."

Bennett took his drink to an overstuffed easy chair and sat down.

"What's this about, Mr. Bennett?"

"I wanted you to see what happens to people who don't accomplish the tasks I set for them."

"And you've got one for me?"

"Yes. I want you to make sure Clint Adams doesn't leave town as soon as he's able."

"And how do I do that?"

"Let him know that the men who shot him are dead," Bennett said. "All of them."

"By who?"

"You."

"He thinks I'm not looking for them."

"Let him know you were," Bennett said. "Let him know you found them and took care of them."

"I can do that," Casey said.

"Yes, well, that's the easy part, isn't it?"

"What's the hard part?"

"Well, killing him, obviously," Bennett said. "Jesus Christ, he was shot . . . how many times?"

"Four."

"And he lived. Remarkable! A remarkable man."

"Yes. What would you like me to do after I've told him?"

Bennett leaned forward.

"Make sure he doesn't leave town."

"Until when?"

Bennett sat back, sipped his brandy, and said, "Until we're ready to try to kill him again."

TEN

"I've been away," Sheriff Mike Casey told Clint Adams. "That's why I haven't been around to see you."

"I just figured you were busy," Clint said.

"Do you want to know where I went?"

"If you want to tell me."

Casey turned and looked at Inga.

"I'm interested," she said. "I saw you ride back in today."

"Did you miss me?"

She smiled but did not answer. Casey turned back to face Clint, who had gotten the feeling there might have been something between him and Inga at one time.

"I went after the men who shot you."

Clint sat up straighter.

"You found out who they were?"

Casey nodded.

"Who?"

"Fella named Cahill and four gunnys he hired. They weren't very good, though."

"Good enough to plug me four times," Clint said. "Where are they?"

"Dead."

"All of them?"

"Yup."

"You killed them?"

"I did."

"Why?"

"Well, first of all, they deserved it. Second, they shot you. Third, they wouldn't come along peaceably."

"But . . . you said you couldn't find them. You said you weren't a detective, remember?"

Casey shrugged.

"I put the word out and found out where one of them was. He led me to the rest."

"But you said you killed them."

"I . . . talked to him first, and he told me where to find the rest of them."

"And then you killed him?"

"Right."

"Why?"

"Like I told you before," Casey said. "He wouldn't come along peaceably. Why all these questions? Didn't you want them killed?"

"If I wanted them killed, I'd kill them myself," Clint said. "What I wanted was at least one of them alive so I could find out who sent them after me."

"I asked them that."

"What'd they say?"

"Nobody sent them," Casey said. "Cahill—he was the leader—he recognized you, and he recruited the others to help him."

"What's Cahill's full name?"

"Ed, Ed Cahill. You know him?"

"Never heard of him. You?"

"Yeah, I've heard a thing or two about him. He was a pretty tough man."

"And the others?"

"They were not as tough, but bad."

"And you killed them all?"

"I sort of got them one, or two, at a time."

Clint relaxed back against his pillows. From that position, from the corner of his eye, he was able to see his gun hanging on the bedpost.

"I guess that makes you a pretty bad man, huh, Sheriff?"

"No," Casey said, "not bad. Why don't I let you get some rest? The Doc says you're comin' along kinda slow."

"Gee," Clint said, "I thought I was doing pretty good for a guy who was shot four times."

The sheriff turned and walked to the door. He opened it and looked back at Clint.

"Shot four times and you survived," he said. "I guess that makes you a pretty bad man."

"No," Clint said, "not bad."

Casey nodded and went out the door. For the first time Clint felt that they understood each other.

ELEVEN

"Tell me about Casey," Clint said to Inga after the sheriff left.

"What about him?"

"Well, why don't you first tell me about you and
him?"

"We were involved . . . once. You could tell?"

"Oh, yeah."

"How."

Clint made some designs in the air with his right fore-
finger and said, "There was something in the air."

"It was over long ago."

"How long?"

"Months."

"That's not so long."

"Are you worried about what he thinks of you and
me?"

"I'm worried about other things."

"Like what?"

"Like him finding and killing five men he said he
wasn't looking for," Clint said. "Like him letting me
know he killed them."

"He was bragging."

"No," Clint said, "he was making a point."

"And what was that?"

"That he's a tough man."

"If you had asked me that I would have told you."

"How long has he been sheriff?"

"A little over a year."

"Who got here first, him or you?"

"I did."

"Do you know what he did before he became sheriff?"

"Not exactly."

"Had he ever been a lawman before?"

"No."

Clint nodded. It was becoming clearer to him.

"Who got here first, Bennett or Casey?"

She thought a moment.

"They got here that close together that you have to think about it?" he asked.

"Yes," she said. "I'm not really sure who was first."

"That's okay," he said, "it doesn't matter. Was Casey elected?"

"What—"

"He wasn't, was he? My guess is the sheriff left mysteriously and Casey was appointed to take his place."

"How did you know that?"

"I didn't," Clint said, "but like I said, I guessed."

"So what does it mean?"

"It means that Casey works for Bennett."

She folded her arms.

"How do you figure that?"

"Bennett used his money twice. Once to get rid of the old sheriff, and then again to put Casey in."

"Why?"

"Because men like him like to have an edge," Clint said. "Having the sheriff work for him gives him that edge."

"Is that how men like him get rich? By having an edge?"

"No," Clint said, "men like him get rich one of two

ways. They either inherit it, or they work damn hard for it. The way they keep it is to always have an edge."

"How do you know so much about rich men?"

"I've met a lot of them."

"How many have you liked?"

"Very few."

"I wonder why?"

"Different reason for each one."

"Why are you disliking Brian Bennett even before you meet him?"

"I'm not, I'm just trying to figure out what I've gotten myself into."

"And what else are you trying to figure out?"

"What do you mean?"

"My guess is," she went on, "you're trying to figure out if I'm involved."

"Involved in what?"

"In whatever it is you think is going on."

Clint stared at her.

"Are you going to ask me?"

"No."

She dropped her arms to her side and walked to the door. "That was the right answer."

"Don't you want to know what I think is going on?"

"Not yet," she said. "I'll give you some more time to think about it."

"And what are you going to do in the meantime?"

"I'm going to try to figure out what it is I've gotten myself into," she said, and left.

Mike Casey was waiting for Inga when she got downstairs.

"Why are you still here?" she asked.

"What did he say after I left?"

"That he was tired and wanted to sleep."

"That's all?"

"Yes."

"It took that long?"

"He was tired. He was speaking slowly."

She tried to move past him, but he grabbed her by the arm and held her tight.

"Let go. You're hurting me."

"Inga—"

"Let . . . go!"

He let her go.

"You're gonna have to pick sides, Inga."

"Why? What's going on, Mike?"

"I'm just warning you," he said. "You're gonna have to pick sides. Think about it."

She didn't say anything. He turned and left. She marveled at how she had come to this country from Sweden to make a new life for herself. She had landed in San Francisco and learned English so well that she almost had no accent left. How had she managed to get from San Francisco to Black Rock without ever having to pick sides before?

And how was she going to get out of Black Rock without doing so now?

TWELVE

Clint stood at the window and watched Sheriff Casey cross the street. He'd obviously been waiting downstairs for Inga to come down. What had he asked her? What had she told him?

Clint had pretty much come to the conclusion that he was in trouble, and there was no one in town he could turn to for help, with the possible exception of Inga. He was still going to have to come to a decision on that one.

He didn't know the whys, but he pretty much figured that somebody wanted him dead. If that wasn't the case, then they never would have allowed the doctor to save his life.

The man with the money was Brian Bennett. Apparently, he'd hired five men to kill him. When they failed, he had his own personal lawman go out and take care of them so none of them could talk. Now the question was, when would they try again, and who would be coming for him when they did? The sheriff? Or someone else yet to be hired?

The name Mike Casey meant nothing to him. He wondered if that was the man's real name or the one he'd taken when he agreed to take the job as sheriff of Black

Rock. He wished he could send another telegram to Rick asking him the same question, but he doubted he'd get such a message past the telegraph clerk.

The only edge he had was that they thought he was recovering more slowly than he was. The doctor had done a very good job of patching him up. Whether or not Milburn was on Bennett's payroll was still up in the air—thought not as up in the air as Inga.

Black Rock was a small town. Could the entire town have been in on it? Was that why nobody saw anything that morning? And why would an entire town cooperate in a scheme to kill him?

Brian Bennett came to town a year ago. What size had it been then? How much had the appearance of his money in town affected it already? Were the towns people willing to do anything to keep him happy?

He didn't know the name Bennett, either. He doubted that the attempt on his life was something personal. Again, if it had been, then the doctor would not have been allowed to save him.

So he didn't know Bennett or Casey, but they knew him. That they knew who he was as soon as he hit town was more than likely.

Right now he was trapped. He was in no condition to get on a horse and leave town. To do so would require some force, and he wasn't even able to sit on a horse, yet. In fact, he was still barely able to make it to the window without being winded. He was pretty sure, though, that nobody was going to come busting into this room to kill him. It appeared likely they were going to wait until he was back on his feet to try again.

Having him killed in town while he was on his own two feet, in some spectacular fashion, would put the town of Black Rock on the map.

Was that what this was about?"

THIRTEEN

When Mike Casey got to his house, he took his gunbelt off and poured himself a shot of whiskey. He drank it, looking out his front window at nothing. He'd been in this town over a year, had done everything that Brian Bennett asked him to do, and what did he have to show for it? A joke of a relationship with a married woman and a little bit of money in the bank.

Brian Bennett had been trying to build Black Rock up ever since he moved here. Casey thought the man had designs on making the town important, and then renaming it Bennettville or something like that. Bennett liked its location between Santa Rosa and Albuquerque, thought it was "advantageous." He had also thought that the arrival of the Gunsmith in their town was "fortuitous." Bennett talked like that, never a small word when a big one would do.

Well, Mike Casey didn't know how fortuitous Clint Adams's presence was anymore. They'd tried for him and failed, and he'd be on his guard after this. Their exchange of machismo in the room hadn't helped any.

Casey wasn't afraid of Clint Adams or his reputation. In fact, he was sure he could take the man. Mike Casey had never seen a man as fast with a gun as he was. He'd always been careful, though, not to let too many other people see it, either. One thing he didn't want was a reputation, or he would have gunned Adams down himself when he first came to town. But that wasn't what he wanted. He wanted money, and a woman to spend it with, and on. He'd thought at one time that the woman would be Inga, but now it seemed to be Gloria—only how was he going to get her away from her husband to live with him on the money he was "paid" by her husband? It seemed very complicated. And did he really want that much grief? How would Bennett take it when he and Gloria ran off together. Of course, if Gloria had her way, Casey would kill Bennett in such a way that she would simply inherit everything.

That was not an option Casey had dismissed. In fact, it might even have been preferable to face Clint Adams with a gun.

Casey finished his drink and poured another. As he did, there was a knock on the back door. He knew it was Gloria. He went into the kitchen and unlocked the back door. As he opened it, she threw herself into his arms. They kissed fiercely and began removing each other's clothes. When he had her naked, he pushed her down on the kitchen table and spread her legs. He got to his knees and buried his face in her fragrant pubic bush, probing with his lips and tongue until she began to pant and shudder. He stood quickly then and drove his rock-hard penis into her with such force he thought the table would collapse. She gasped, brought her legs up and wrapped them around him, her heels against his buttocks, and held on for dear life.

Later, they moved to the bedroom and made love this time—rather than simply having sex, which was what they had done on the kitchen table.

"Did you do it?" she asked in his ear.

"Yes."

"Then it's over."

"Yes," he lied, and then added, "for now . . ."

She didn't hear that part. She only heard what she wanted to hear. When he entered her again, she pulled his head down so she could kiss him, and from that point on all she could hear was the beat of her heart.

Later, she replayed the scene in her mind and realized what he had said.

"What did you mean, for now?" she asked as they lay together.

"It's over until Adams recovers and gets back on his feet."

"And then what?"

"That will be up to your husband."

"Damn it," she said, "why can't we take control of our lives, Mike?"

"Gloria—"

"I know you're not afraid of him."

"No, I'm not."

"Then what is it? Loyalty?"

"Maybe."

"For what?" she asked. "Once he's finished with you, he'll discard you. He feels no loyalty to you."

"I know that."

"He hates you, if you must know the truth."

"Does he know—?"

"About us? No. He hates you because you're everything he wishes he was. You're young, tall, good looking, and not afraid of anything."

"He's not afraid—"

"Don't let him fool you," she said. "He's afraid of everything. He just thinks his money protects him from everything."

"And it doesn't?"

"No, it doesn't," she said. "Maybe from most things, but not from everything."

"Like what?"

"Like you, baby," she said, "like me. Like us and what we can do."

"You're talking about killing him again."

"Yes, I am. Just think about it, that's all I ask. Think about it . . . later." She put her hands on him, brought his body to life. "Come here," she said. "Come here . . ."

Later, when she was gone and he was in bed alone with her scent, he did think about it. He thought about it long and hard.

FOURTEEN

Clint was awake when Inga came in with his breakfast.

"Did you sleep well last night?" she asked.

"I slept fine," he said. "How about you?"

She set the tray on his lap, as he had gotten into the habit of feeding himself.

"No, I did not sleep fine."

"And why's that?" he asked. "Something to do with Mike Casey?"

"What about him?"

"I saw him leave yesterday," he said, before he realized that this would give away the fact that he had been at the window. He hoped she wouldn't catch on. "That means you and he talked before he left."

"Yes, we did."

"About what?"

"He told me I was going to have to be prepared to choose sides."

"Between him and me?"

"He didn't say exactly," she said, "but that's when I decided that I have to leave here."

"And when will that be?"

"I will leave when you do."

He had some coffee and set the cup down.

"I don't know if it's anybody's intention to let me leave here, Inga," he said. "My advice to you is to go, if you really want to."

"I . . . I want to sell this place first," she said. "I can't just leave it. And I don't want to leave you alone."

"Are you prepared to pick up a gun to help me?"

"I've never fired a gun."

"Then there's no point in staying," he said. "You can't help me with what I have to do, and I'll probably end up getting killed if I have to worry about you."

"I can't just leave. Everything I have is tied up in this place."

"You have an alternative."

"What is that?"

"Stay, and choose the other side."

She bit her lip.

"I'm not sure who is on the other side."

"Take it from me," he said. "Everybody is. If you stand by me you'll end up taking on the whole town, and you don't want to do that."

"The whole town?"

"Or most of it," he said. "That's my feeling."

"How can you go against an entire town?"

"Well, as long as I stay in this room," he said, chewing a piece of bacon, "I won't have to. It's when I'm well enough to walk out that I'll have the problem."

"Wait a minute," she said. "You just said you saw Casey leave yesterday. That means . . . you went to the window?"

"You caught me."

"You can get up?"

"I've been walking around for a few days," he said, "just trying to get my legs back."

"What would have happened if you'd fallen?" she asked. "You could have opened your wounds."

"I didn't fall," he said.

"Why are you risking injury—"

"Inga," he said, "I'm going to confide in you now, knowing that if you don't choose my side, you'll be able to do me great harm."

"I've already chosen, Clint," she said. "I don't want to side with them. That only leaves you."

"Or you could leave, thereby taking your own side."

"I . . . I can't just leave."

"All right," he said. "I have to try to get myself ready well before the doctor is predicting. No one can know that I've been on my feet already."

"I understand," she said. "You're pretending to progress more slowly to throw them off guard."

"That's right."

"But once you're on your feet, what can you do against so many?" she asked.

"Not much," he said, "not alone."

"But . . . who will help you?"

"Inga," he said, eating some more bacon, "that's something you and I are going to have to work on."

FIFTEEN

Clint knew that the telegraph message was going to have to be worded very carefully. If, as he suspected, most of the town was in on this, the telegraph clerk would have to report back to Sheriff Casey on whatever was sent out.

Inga brought Clint a pencil and some paper and waited while he figured out what he wanted to write.

"This could get you in trouble, Inga," he said. "I mean, taking this over to the telegraph office."

"I know," she said.

"Casey will see this as your signal as to which side you're taking."

"Probably."

"That doesn't bother you?"

"Mike wouldn't hurt me."

"You're sure of that?"

"Yes."

"And what about Bennett?"

"I'm not sure about him," she said, "but Mike would not let him hurt me, either."

Clint finished writing and reread it before giving it to Inga.

"I hate making you take a chance like this."

"You're not making me," she said. "This is my choice."

"All right," he said, "wait until it's late, just before the office closes, and then go over and send it. Does the clerk know you?"

"Yes, he does."

"Is he old or young?"

"Why does that matter?"

"Well, if he's young he probably has a crush on you."

"And you think I only appeal to young men?"

"Well, no," he said, "I think you appeal to all men, but—"

"Never mind," she said. "He is young, and he will send it for me."

"Good."

"In fact," she said, "if it *was* me . . ."

"What are you thinking?"

"If the message was from me and I asked him not to tell anyone," she said, "I think he would go along with it."

"That's an idea," Clint said. "In fact, as long as it's not from me I'll bet he'd send it without saying anything about it. After all, he's probably been told to be on the look out for telegrams from me."

"Then we should rewrite it," she said.

"You should write it so that it sounds like it's from a woman."

"But how will your friend know it's from you?"

"He's already gotten one from me from this town," Clint said, "and he doesn't know you. Getting a telegram from you will make him suspicious."

"Then does it really matter what it says?"

"Actually," Clint said, "not as much. Okay, take the pencil and just send this."

Doing as she was told, Inga waited until just before clos-ing and then walked over to the telegraph office. The clerk—whose name was Bobby—did indeed have a crush on Inga, for he was in his early twenties and did not have much experience with women. Although Inga was six or eight years older than he was, he found her to be the prettiest woman in town.

"Hello, Miss Inga."

"Hi, Bobby."

"Can I help you?"

"I just have a short telegram to send, Bobby," she said. "I'd really appreciate it. I know it's almost closing time."

"Oh, that's okay, Miss Inga," he said. "Anything for you."

She leaned over the counter to give him the message, so he'd get a whiff of the extra perfume she'd put on. She hoped to distract him enough that he wouldn't realize where the message was going.

She decided to lay it on thick and touched his hand.

"Your hand is so graceful," she said. "I love the way it works the telegraph key."

"Aw, there ain't that much to it," he said, blushing.

"May I come around the counter and stand behind you to watch?"

"Well . . . sure. I don't see why not."

She came around the counter, and as he sat down at the key, she stood behind him, put both hands on his shoulders, and then leaned against him so he could feel her body heat. He *was* kind of cute, and it wasn't such a chore to flirt with him. She actually found herself enjoying it.

He started to send the message, and she leaned over so that her face was right next to his, her breath on his ear. Bobby had such an erection that he found it hard to concentrate on sending the message. He had to concentrate more on not messing his pants.

"There," he said, relieved that he'd managed to accomplish both tasks. "It's done."

"That's all there was to it?" she asked.

"That's all, Ma'am."

She rubbed his back with one hand, teasing him some more. While leaning over she'd been able to see his lap and knew that he was aroused. Truth be told, so was she. Under other, more innocent circumstances . . .

"Well, thank you, Bobby," she said. "You've been really sweet."

"It was n-nothing . . . r-really . . ."

She leaned over and kissed his cheek gently. He had peach fuzz on his face rather than beard stubble.

"I have to go," she said. "Thank you. Don't get up. Have a nice evening."

"Yes, Ma'am, you, too."

Bobby couldn't have gotten up if he wanted to. He was right on the verge of messing his pants. He waited for Inga to leave the office, then stood up slowly, thinking that would possibly enable him to alleviate the problem without a mess.

He was wrong.

SIXTEEN

In Labyrinth, Texas, the telegraph operator carried the message to Rick's Place, the saloon and gambling hall run by Clint's friend, Rick Hartman. The operator found Rick seated at his private table in the back of the room with a guest.

"Telegram for you, Mr. Hartman."

"Thanks, Cal."

Hartman read it, then read it again.

"A problem?" his guest asked.

"I don't know," Hartman said. "It's from a woman in Black Rock, New Mexico."

"Never heard of it."

"I hadn't, either, until a little over a week ago. That's where the message came from Clint, saying he'd been shot."

"Two telegrams from the same obscure place in a week's time?" the guest asked. "What's this one say?"

"It's gibberish," Hartman said. "Something about a dress order, and it's signed Inga Swenson."

"Do you know an Inga Swenson?"

"Never heard of her."

"What do you make of it?"

Hartman put the message down.

"I haven't heard from Clint in over a week, not since the first time," Hartman said. "It sounded like he'd been pretty badly hurt, but his first message said he'd be all right."

"Did it occur to you to go there and find out?"

Hartman looked away from his guest. The man was also good friends with Clint Adams, probably a better friend than Rick himself. Hartman *had* thought about going to Black Rock, but the truth was he rarely left Labyrinth anymore, and Clint's message *had* said that he'd be all right.

"Never mind," the other man said. "Can I see that?"

"Sure." Hartman handed it over.

"I don't see any hidden messages in here," the other man said. "Apparently, the fact that it was sent is a hidden message in itself."

He handed it back to Hartman and stood up.

"What are you going to do?" Hartman asked.

"I'm going to Black Rock."

"I'll come with you."

"You better stay here."

"Why?"

"Because if Clint does need help and needs to contact someone again, it will be you."

Hartman settled back in his chair.

"Don't worry," Bat Masterson said, "I'll get to the bottom of this."

SEVENTEEN

The next morning, when Inga came into the room, Clint was standing by the window. She gave him a stern look, but said nothing. Clint decided he'd gone too far not to trust her now, so there was no need to hide the fact that he was on his feet.

"How do you feel?"

"Better," he said.

"Do you want breakfast today?"

"Just some coffee—but wait. What happened last night? You didn't come back and tell me."

"I did," she said, "but you were asleep. That's the best thing for you, so I didn't want to wake you."

Clint was already annoyed that he'd slept so soundly last night. He'd awakened with a start, reaching for his gun, only to find himself alone in the room. He was pleased, however, that the sudden move toward his gun had not resulted in any pain from his wounds.

"Well?"

"The message went out," she said, "and I believe I distracted the clerk enough so that he won't say anything."

"What makes you think that?"

"It would be . . . somewhat embarrassing to him if he had to tell the whole story."

"Makes me wish I'd been there to see it."

"It made me wish you were awake when I got back," she said, "and healthy."

"Sounds like flirting agrees with you."

"It's not something I do a lot."

She certainly had not flirted with him. It had been a simple matter of eyes locking and sending the same message.

"Watch," he said, and started away from the window.

"Easy," she said, but he was walking gently, yet firmly toward her.

When he reached her he said, "I just want a hug—a light one."

He put his arms out and she came into them. She carefully put her arms around him, avoiding contact with his wounds, and they stood that way for a while, cheek to cheek, sharing the warmth of their bodies.

"Mmmm," he said, disengaging from her, "thank you."

She took his face in her hands and kissed his mouth gently. Quickly, the kiss deepened, and he put his arms around her again. She slid her arms up his back, and he hissed involuntarily when she brushed the wound high on the left side.

"Oh, I'm sorry!" she said, jumping back.

"It's okay," he said, backing away a few steps. "We'll just have to control ourselves a little longer."

"Sit on the bed and let me check your dressings," she ordered, and he complied.

She checked each of them carefully, spending even more time on the one she had made contact with.

"How am I?" he asked.

"Everything looks fine."

"There, see?" he said. "No harm done."

"We were lucky," she said. "There, you're finished. Now, get back into bed."

"I wanted to walk around a bit—"

"Get in bed and rest," she said, firmly. "That is the most important thing of all."

He did as she asked, and she pulled the covers up over him.

"I'll get you some coffee."

"I'll wait here."

"Don't get up."

"I won't."

She left and returned shortly with a pot of coffee and two cups. True to his word, he had not gotten up out of bed.

"I thought I would have a cup with you."

"Good idea."

She poured two cups and handed him his. Then she pulled a chair over and sat by him, holding her cup.

"I have a question."

"Ask it."

"What happens if your friend Rick sends a telegram back saying he doesn't know who I am?"

"What would the clerk do with such a telegram?"

"He would bring it to me, I suppose."

"Then it wouldn't matter, as long as no one else saw it."

"But, wouldn't that mean that he didn't understand?" Clint frowned.

"I see what you mean—but I don't think that will happen. Rick is smart. He'll figure it out."

"And then what will he do?" she asked. "Will he come here to help you?"

Clint thought for a moment. Rich Hartman left Labyrinth less and less these days, and it was getting to the point where Clint thought it might be some sort of phobia.

"I don't think so," he said. "He'll probably send someone."

"Who?"

"I don't know."

"One person?"

"I don't know that, either," Clint said. "He'll send whoever is closest, I suppose."

"A gunman friend of yours, perhaps?"

"Inga, gunmen are just men, like everybody else."

She held her cup in both hands, sipped from it thoughtfully, and then said, "I don't think so."

"How many gunmen have you known?"

"Just one," she said, staring at him, "and he's like no other man I ever met."

EIGHTEEN

When Mike Casey came out of the sheriff's office that morning, he was surprised to see Brian Bennett riding into town in a buggy. Bennett almost never came to town. He wondered what could be bringing him in today.

He crossed the street to where Bennett's driver had stopped the buggy and stood by while Bennett stepped down. The man was dressed impeccably in a three-piece suit and a bowler hat. His beard was carefully trimmed and even his hands looked perfect, but there was nothing he could do about the fact that he most resembled a gnome.

"Mr. Bennett," Casey greeted.

"Ah, Mike," Bennett said. "Good to see you."

Casey learned long ago—and never as pointedly as just the other day—that Bennett could smile at you and sound as congenial as could be and then strike at you with the speed of a rattler. He'd make you feel like you were his best friend, but if you crossed him, or even just disappointed him . . .

"What brings you to town?" Casey asked.

"Just some business at the bank, today, Mike," Bennett said. "Nothing to concern you."

73

"Are you making a withdrawal or deposit? Do you need me to walk with you?"

"No, no," Bennett said, "I have Earl, here. I'm very secure with him."

Casey looked at Earl Benjamin, who he knew to be Bennett's driver. He didn't know anything else about the man, though, except that he appeared formidable and imperturbable. He dressed as his boss did, but it was obvious that he had a gun in a shoulder rig under his jacket.

"Well," Casey said, "if there's anything I can do for you . . ."

"Actually, Mike," Bennett said, touching his pursed lips with his index finger, "there is something I want you to do for me."

"Oh, what's that?"

"After I'm finished with my banking," Bennett said, "I'd like you to take me to the hotel and introduce me to our guest."

"Guest?"

"Yes," Bennett said, "Clint Adams, the famous Gunsmith."

"You . . . want to meet him?"

"Yes, I do," Bennett said. He leaned toward Casey so only the lawman could hear him. "I consider it rude to have a man killed without having met him first."

Casey didn't know what to say.

"You'll take care of that for me, won't you, Sheriff?" Bennett said, aloud.

"Uh, sure, Mr. Bennett," Casey said, still puzzled, "I'll, uh, introduce you."

"Thank you," Bennett said. "I'll see you in your office in a few minutes, then. Earl? To the bank."

NINETEEN

"He wants to what?" Doctor Milburn said.

"He wants to meet Adams."

"What the hell for?"

"I don't know," Casey said. "Some nonsense about not having a man killed until he meets him first."

"That didn't stop him from sending five men to kill him last week, did it?" the doctor asked.

"I guess this is something new for him," Casey said. "Meeting a famous gunman. Is Adams up to this?"

"What does he have to do but lie in bed and receive Bennett?" Milburn asked. "I'm sure he can handle it."

"All right," Casey said. "I'll go back to my office and wait for Bennett to show up."

"Come by and get me, Mike," Milburn said. "I'll go up with you to see him. This is something I don't want to miss."

"Okay," Casey said. "I'll tell him that you were going up to check on him, anyway. He'll like your devotion to duty."

"Who cares what he likes?" Milburn asked. "The man's a buffoon. If it wasn't for his money . . ."

"But he does have money, doesn't he, Doc?" Casey asked. He didn't bother telling the doctor that he didn't

consider the man such a buffoon—not after the way
Bennett had dispassionately dispatched Ed Cahill.

"Yeah, he's got money," Milburn said, sourly, "that's
how we all got into this mess in the first place."

Casey was behind his desk when Brian Bennett came
walking in, with Earl behind him. Mike Casey couldn't
recall ever having heard Earl speak a word.

"Are we ready, Sheriff?" Bennett asked.

"I'm ready," Casey said. "We got to swing by to get
the doctor. He was planning on going up to check on
Adams, anyway."

"No problem," Bennett said. "The more, the merrier.
I'm looking forward to seeing the lovely Miss Swenson."

"She'll be there," Casey said. "She's been a very at-
tentive nurse."

Bennett chuckled.

"He's a lucky man to have her as his nurse," the man
said. "Shall we go?"

"Is Earl coming, too?"

"Of course," Bennett said. "Earl goes everywhere I
go. He's not just my driver now, but my bodyguard."

"You feel you need a bodyguard now, Mr. Bennett?"

"One never knows, Sheriff," Bennett said, "one never
knows."

TWENTY

Inga was surprised when Sheriff Casey came walking into her shop with Doctor Milburn, another man she didn't know, and Brian Bennett.

"Gentlemen," she said. "Can I help you?"

"Miss Swenson," Bennett said, with magnanimous good manners. "What a pleasure to see you."

"Hello, Mr. Bennett."

Bennett executed a bow that would have looked sophisticated coming from another man. From him it just looked comical. She tried to hide her revulsion as he took her hand and kissed it.

"I understand you have been Mr. Adams's nurse since the, uh, unfortunate incident."

"Yes," she said, "I'm trying to do my part."

"You and the good doctor have kept him alive, I've been told."

"I'm sure the doctor has done that all by himself, Mr. Bennett. Is there something I can do for you? Something you or your wife needs from my shop, perhaps?"

"No," Bennett said, "actually, I'm here to visit Mr. Adams."

"Visit him?"

"Yes," Bennett said. "After all, he's a guest in our

town, and he's been treated pretty rudely. In fact, I think
the Mayor should be here as well."

"Mr. Bennett?" Casey said.

"Yes, Sheriff?"

"Uh, as of last month, you are the Mayor, sir."

"Oh, that's right," Bennett said. "It slipped my mind.
Well then, why don't we go up and see him?"

"Excuse me," Inga said, "but may I go up and tell
him you're coming? After all, he might be asleep."

"Inga," Casey said, "I don't think Mr. Bennett wants
to—"

"No, no, Sheriff," Bennett said, "the young lady is
quite right. By all means, Miss Swenson, go up and, uh,
prepare Mr. Adams for my visit. We'll wait down here
until you call for us."

"Thank you, Mr. Bennett," Inga said. "That's very
nice of you."

"Not at all."

Inga turned, went through a curtained doorway and
then up the stairs to the second floor.

"She's going to warn him," Casey said.

Bennett turned and looked at the sheriff.

"I'm not here to ambush the man, Sheriff," Bennett
said, "I just want to meet him and talk to him. We'll all
just wait here, like I said."

Inga knocked on Clint's door and entered.

"Oh good," she said, when he looked at her, "you're
awake. Have you been to the window?"

"No, why?"

"There are some men downstairs to see you."

"Who?"

"The sheriff, the doctor, and Brian Bennett."

"Bennett himself is here?"

"With another man I don't know. A big man."

"What's it about?"

"Well, he *says* that you're a guest in Black Rock and been treated rudely."

Clint laughed aloud.

"Oh, send them up, sweetheart," he said. "This sounds like it could be a lot of fun."

"Clint . . . what if they're here to kill you?"

"I don't think Bennett and the sheriff would be so obvious, Inga. Bennett probably just wants to take a look at me. Wait, I've got an idea."

Clint took his gun from his holster and slid it under his blanket.

"Take the holster off the bedpost and put it in a drawer."

She did as he told her.

"Now let me slide down here so I look like I'm on my deathbed."

Inga got the idea and went to the bed to slide his pillows beneath his head.

"Do you think this will work?" she asked.

"I don't know, Inga," he said, "I'm just trying to have some fun with it. How do I look?"

She stepped back to evaluate his appearance, told him to close his eyes a bit, then said, "Yes, you look . . . terrible."

"Bring them up, darlin'."

TWENTY-ONE

Inga opened the door, entered the room first and said, "Come in, gentlemen."

Before anyone could move, Bennett put his hand out to stop the doctor from entering.

"We don't want to crowd the man, Doctor. You can examine him after I've spoken with him."

Milburn looked at Casey, who simply shrugged.

"Very well," the doctor said. "I'll wait out here."

"What about me?" Casey asked Bennett.

"Of course you can come in, Sheriff," Bennett said. "You're the law, aren't you?"

"Earl?"

Bennett's man, Earl, entered first, then stepped aside to let his boss enter. Sheriff Casey brought up the rear. They all looked at Clint Adams, who was lying flat on his back with his bedcovers up to his neck. Casey—who had previously seen the gunbelt hanging on the bed-post—noticed that Adams's gun was nowhere in sight, nor was the holster. He had to bite back a smile.

"Mr. Adams," he said, "this is Mr. Brian Bennett. He is the Mayor of Black Rock."

Clint turned his head to look at the Mayor.

"Nice to meet you, Mayor." His voice was faint.

"I'm sorry I didn't get up here to visit you earlier, Mr. Adams," Bennett said. "I'm also sorry that you've come to harm in our town. I hope you won't hold it against all of Black Rock."

"Of course not," Clint said. "How could an entire town be responsible for one act?"

"Exactly."

Clint had his eye specifically on the big, quiet man in the room. He could see the bulge of a shoulder rig beneath his jacket.

"I'm sorry," Bennett said, "I'm being rude. This is my driver, Earl."

"Nice to meet you," Clint said.

Earl might have nodded, but Clint couldn't be sure.

"I just wanted you to know that you may have anything you need in our town," Bennett said. "I know you'll eventually need a hotel room. I assure you, you won't be charged for it."

"I appreciate that, Mr. Bennett."

"I'm sure you know that our fine sheriff has diligently hunted down the men who shot you and has meted our the justice they so richly deserved."

"Really?" Clint asked. "I thought he just killed them."

Bennett smiled. "Well, that's the justice we felt they deserved."

Clint was still watching Earl. If a move was going to come from anyone, it would be him, and he was prepared to fire at the man from beneath the covers.

Bennett looked around. "Do you have everything you need here?"

"I'm fine," Clint said. "I have a great nurse."

"Yes, you do."

"And a fine doctor. I thought he was with you?"

"You're right," Bennett said, "the doctor is a fine physician. He's out in the hall, waiting to come in and examine you. We won't take up any more of your time. I just wanted you to know how outraged I was at what happened. I'm sure a man of your reputation is used to being shot at, but this . . . this ambush by four or five men was just . . . appalling."

"I couldn't agree with you more, sir."

"Miss Swenson?" Bennett said. "You continue to take good care of our guest."

"Oh, I will, Mr. Bennett, I will."

"Sheriff?"

Casey turned and opened the door.

"Doctor?" Bennett said. "He's all yours, now."

Bennett went out first, followed by Earl, and then by Casey, who threw one last amused glance Clint's way before leaving.

"I'll see you gentlemen out," Inga said. She looked at Clint and said, "I'll be back."

As she left, the doctor came in and closed the door.

"What was that all about?" he asked.

"I guess he just wanted to apologize."

"Well," the doctor said, approaching the bed, "let's have a look at you."

The doctor pulled down Clint's bedclothes and was startled to see the gun in Clint's hand.

"You had that the whole time?" he asked.

"Well, doctor," Clint said, "you never can be too careful, you know?"

TWENTY-TWO

The doctor checked Clint's wounds and found them clean and free of infection.

"Inga's doing a good job with these dressings," he said. "She probably should be a nurse."

"So tell me, Doctor," Clint said, "why do you think Mr. Bennett came up here?"

"The truth?"

"Please."

"I haven't the faintest idea," Milburn said. "The man does whatever he wants, and it never makes very much sense to me."

"When did he become mayor? This was the first I heard of it."

"Last month," Milburn said. "Our Mayor decided to leave down overnight, and the town council appointed Mr. Bennett mayor."

"Who sits on the council?"

"Several businessmen in town," Milburn said, "myself and Mr. Bennett."

"I see. And did Mr. Bennett have a vote?"

"He did," the doctor said. "Like I said, he's a member of the council."

"And did you vote?"

The doctor finished with the last of Clint's dressings and sat back in his chair to survey his handiwork.

"I'm afraid I abstained from voting," he said. "You can lie back down, if you like."

"Would you help me with these pillows? I think I'd like to try sitting up. I'll probably make a better impression next time I get paid a visit."

"Sure."

Milburn adjusted the pillows and helped Clint sit back.

"It's probably good that you're sitting up," he said, closing his black bag. "Maybe next week you can even try standing."

"I'll look forward to that."

"I don't see any reason for me to come back until the end of the week," Milburn said. "If you need me before then, have Inga come and get me."

"All right, Doctor," Clint said. "And thanks."

The doctor started for the door, but stopped when Clint called out his name.

"The Mayor said I could have anything in town I wanted . . . for free," he said.

"And?"

"I was just wondering," Clint said, "if that included your services."

"I'll give you a bill for my services, Mr. Adams," Milburn said. "It will be quite up to you if you wish to pay it."

As Milburn opened the door, Inga appeared in the doorway. She and the doctor exchanged a few words, and then he left and she closed the door.

"Want do you think?" Clint asked.

"I think you should be an actor," she said. "You gave a great performance. You fooled everyone."

"Not everyone."

"Oh? Who didn't you fool?"

"The sheriff."

"How could you tell?"

"It was all he could do to keep from laughing."

"And why is that?"

"He knew I had the gun under the blanket. He probably remembered from other visits that it had been hanging on the bedpost."

"Will he tell Bennett, I wonder?"

"I wonder, too."

"What did the doctor say about your wounds?"

"He's very impressed with your nursing skills," Clint said. "He helped me sit up and said that I might even try standing next week."

"Well, I guess he's fooled."

"Anything happen downstairs when they left?"

"No," she said. "I showed them to the door, and they all went to the sheriff's office together. I, uh, watched them from my window."

"Well," Clint said, "I would like to be a fly on the wall of that office right now."

TWENTY-THREE

"He looked like he could hardly move," Bennett said when they reached the sheriff's office.

"Well," Casey said, "he *was* shot four times."

"What did you think, Earl?" Bennett asked, looking at the other man.

Casey thought he was finally going to get a chance to hear Earl speak, but the big man and the small man seemed to be able to communicate without benefit of speech.

"Earl doesn't think Adams looked so tough. I might decide to let Earl have a try at him when he's back on his feet."

"That would be up to you."

"You don't think Earl would have a chance against the Gunsmith, Sheriff?" Bennett asked.

"No, sir," Casey said. "I don't think Earl would have a chance in hell against the Gunsmith or anyone else who was decent with a gun and wearing a western rig. Not with that shoulder rig he's got on."

"Earl's very good, Mike."

"If you say so, sir."

"Earl," Bennett said, "it's time we got back to the ranch." Bennett looked at Casey. "It looks to me like we've got plenty of time before we have to decide what to do about Clint Adams."

"You just let me know when you decide, Mr. Bennett," Casey said. "After all, you're the boss."

"How nice that you remember that, Sheriff."

After Earl and Brian Bennett left the sheriff's office, Casey walked over to see if the doc had returned to his.

"He had a gun under the bed covers the whole time," Milburn said as Casey walked in.

Casey laughed. "I know that."

"How did you know?"

"Doc, it's my business to know."

"Come on, come on," Milburn said. "How'd you know?"

"He's been keeping his holster hanging on the bedpost," Casey said.

"So?"

"So it wasn't there today. When Inga went up to tell him that Bennett was there to see him, I'm sure he had her hide the holster so he could palm his gun beneath the covers."

"Why didn't he use it?"

"What for? He didn't feel threatened. It was only there in case he needed it."

"He's a careful man."

"Very careful. Tell me, Doc. Is he as bad off as he looked today?"

"What do you mean?"

"He seemed to hardly be able to move."

"Well, I had to help him sit up after I finished checking his wounds."

"And how are his wounds?"

"Nice and clean. They're healing. Next week he can start trying to get to his feet."

"Yeah," Casey said, scratching the stubble on his face.

He hadn't shaved that morning. "That is, unless he's already walking."

"Are we going to go through this again, Mike? I'm the doctor, you're the lawman."

"I'm thinking like a lawman, Doc," Casey said. "I'm suspicious. I think maybe he's not as bad off as he'd like us to think."

"Why do you say that?"

"Well," Casey said, "it seems to me that would be his only edge over us."

"Why would he think he needs an edge over us?"

"Doc, do you think he buys that five men attacked him without being sent, and that I went out and hunted them down and took care of them for him?"

"Isn't that what he's supposed to think?"

"I don't think Clint Adams ever says, does, or thinks what people expect him to," Casey said.

"Well, what's the difference?" Milburn said. "He's still all alone in town. What harm could he do?"

"A man like him? A hell of a lot."

"I think you're being too suspicious, Sheriff."

"Maybe," Casey said. "Maybe. I'll see you later, Doc."

"Yeah," Milburn said, sourly. "See you later."

Mike Casey left the doctor's office and went right back to his own. He sat behind his desk, put his feet up, and thought again about how the Gunsmith looked when they all entered his room. He laughed out loud. Clint Adams was quite a character. He wondered what would have happened if Bennett had given Earl the word and the big man had gone for his gun. Earl was a joker in this deck. He had not given the man any respect when Bennett asked about it because he'd wanted to see what Earl would do. It didn't seem to faze the man. Casey decided that he could probably take Earl, but he wouldn't look forward to having the opportunity to find out.

He was making himself a pot of coffee when his office door opened and a young man came walking in.

"Can I talk to you for a minute, Sheriff?"

"Sure, Bobby," Casey said. "Come on in. I was just making some coffee. Want some?"

"Uh, no sir."

"Well then, what's on your mind?"

"Uh, somethin' that happened yesterday," Bobby said, "when I was working at the telegraph office. . . ."

TWENTY-FOUR

After Bobby left, Mike Casey pondered what he had been told. Bobby even showed him a copy of the telegraph message. For Inga to send it made no sense at all, and neither did what it said. The only answer was that it wasn't supposed to make sense. It must have been some kind of signal from Clint Adams. The fact that he'd even send a signal, and that Inga would send it for him, changed things quite a bit. This was something he was going to have to talk to Ed Milburn about. After that, maybe he'd fill Bennett in as well.

Inga was looking out the front window of her shop when the clerk, Bobby, came out of the sheriff's office. Apparently, the effect of her charms had worn off, and Bobby had told Mike Casey about her telegram.

She went back upstairs to talk to Clint.

Ed Milburn was sitting at his desk in his office, turning the situation over in his mind. It went against his Hippocratic oath to nurse a man back to help and then help kill him. The idea of killing Adams to put Black Rock on the map seemed a sound one at the time it had been conceived. After all, Adams was just a gunman, and a whole town would benefit from his death. The only tricky part had been persuading Brian Bennett not only to pay for it, but that it was his idea in the first place.

But Adams hadn't died, and now things were getting complicated. So what if Adams had died in bed of complications? He still would have been shot to death in Black Rock, right? All Milburn would have had to do was slip while removing one of the bullets—but planning a man's death was one thing, killing him yourself quite another . . . especially for a doctor.

But there was no choice, now. Clint Adams had to die before he caught on to what was happening. The question was, how and where?

And who would do it?

"I'm worried," Inga said as she entered the room.

"About what? The sheriff? If he was going to give me away, he would have done it sooner."

"No," she said, "I'm not worried about that. I mean, yes, it's the sheriff, but not that. I just saw the telegraph clerk coming out of the sheriff's office."

"Oh," Clint said. "You think the effects of your flirtation have worn off? Is that it?"

"Yes."

"And what will Sheriff Casey do?"

"I don't know."

"Well," Clint said, "we can't take any chances. I think you should close your shop, Inga."

"What?"

"And stay inside. We'll both be safe as long as we're in here."

"I can't close the shop," she said. "How will I live? I mean, it's a struggle as it is, but if I close—"

"Just until this is over," he said. "Besides, weren't you talking about leaving?"

"Yes, but I still have to make a living while I'm here."

"First you have to live, Inga."

"Mike won't kill me."

"Then what are you worried about?"

"I'm worried how it might affect you, not me," she said.

"Oh." Suddenly, he felt very dense.

"If they figure out that you sent a signal, they'll *have* to do something, maybe even come after you."

"You have a point," he said, "but that's all the more reason why you should close. Let's not make it easy for anyone to get in here. Maybe Mike Casey won't hurt you, but Brian Bennett has other men on his payroll . . . like that fella Earl. There's a killer if I ever saw one."

"Earl? He drives Mr. Bennett. I've never even heard him speak."

"Those are the ones you have to worry about, Inga," Clint said. "The quiet ones with guns under their arms."

"A gun? Under his arm?"

"In a shoulder holster."

"But how do you know?"

"That's how I stay alive, Inga," Clint said. "By noticing things like that."

"I see."

"What about closing the shop?"

"All right," she said, "but just for a while."

"Go on down and lock up, then come back here. I think we should stay in the same room from now on, too."

"The same room? And the same bed?"

"There is only one."

"But you can't—"

"We can *sleep* in the bed together, Inga, and do nothing else. After all, we are adults, aren't we?"

"Of course."

"Go on, then. Lock the doors and come back up. We can watch the street from the window."

"All right," she said. "I'll be right back."

After she left, Clint started to worry about Duke. The

big gelding was very vulnerable locked up in the livery
the way he was. He just hoped nobody decided to harm
him.

That would *really* make him mad.

TWENTY-FIVE

Mike Casey stuck his head in Doc Milburn's door.

"Get a drink?"

"You buyin'?"

"Why not?"

"Let's go."

When they were seated at a table with their beers, Casey told Milburn about Inga's message.

"What is she tryin' to pull?" the doc asked.

"I told her she was going to have to take sides," Casey said. "I guess she has."

"What does she think is gonna happen when he finds out she was in on it from the beginning?"

"Maybe she's not thinking that far ahead," Casey said.

"Why is she takin' his side, anyway?" Milburn demanded. "Ain't she part of this town?"

"We're all part of this town, Doc."

"Well, she don't act like it."

They drank some beer in silence, each alone with his own thoughts for a while, but not quite alone.

"Whatever happened to you and her?" Milburn asked.

"I think you know."

"Jesus," the doctor said, "you and Gloria? Still?"

"Still."

"What are you gonna do when Bennett finds out?"

"She wants me to kill him."

Milburn stared at him.

"You aren't gonna do it, are you?"

"No," the lawman said, "at least, not until we're finished with him."

"Well, shit, after we're done you can do what you want to him," Ed Milburn said. "That little gnome gives me the creeps. Can you imagine Gloria letting him touch her?"

"I try not to."

"Oh, sorry. . . ."

Again they lapsed into silence.

"You ever think about leavin' here?" Milburn asked.

"Sure."

"And what happens?"

"I stop thinking about it."

"Why?"

"I didn't like it out there, Ed."

"But you like it here?"

"A lot."

"But you want this place to change, don't you? Grow bigger?"

Casey didn't answer right away.

"Mike?"

"I don't know," Casey said. "If it gets bigger, we'll have the same kind of problems everyone else has."

"But . . . you agreed to go along with this. To try to help Black Rock grow."

"Everybody else wanted it."

"But not you."

Casey sighed.

"I guess if it gets too big I can move on."

"So you move on and Bennett stays? That's not the kind of trade I want to make."

Casey pushed away his partially finished beer and

stared across the table at the only man in town he truly thought of as a friend.

"Don't worry, Ed," he said. "I'll do my part to help Black Rock grow."

"Then here's to doin' our part," Milburn said.

Sheriff Mike Casey picked his beer up and said, "Okay, here's to doin' our part."

TWENTY-SIX

"Do you know why I like you, Earl?" Brian Bennett asked.

Earl sat across from Bennett in his den, as silent as ever. In fact, Bennett had even started thinking of him as "Silent Earl."

"Because you're silent."

Earl stared.

"You listen while I talk. That's a lost art, my silent friend, let me tell you."

Earl raised his eyebrows.

"And I can think out loud with you."

Earl lowered his eyebrows.

"Do you know what I'm thinking now?"

Earl even managed to shake his head with his eyes.

"I'm thinking that Mike Casey and Ed Milburn think they're real smart. They even think they're smarter than me. But you know what? They're not. They think they're using me, but they're the ones being used. After all, I'd never be able to control the town council without them. Once I have what I want, though, I won't need them anymore. And then, my friend, they're going to be all yours."

Was that a smile? Bennett didn't think so. If Earl ever

smiled, he'd fire him. He liked Earl just the way he was.

"And another thing," he said. "The handsome young sheriff doesn't think I know he's sleeping with my wife."

Earl frowned now, his most frightening expression.

"Oh yes, I've known about it for some time. And do you know what? I don't care. They're keeping each other occupied, that's all. In the end, they'll all be gone and I'll be here, and I'll be in charge. Black Rock will be mine, and then I'll change the name. Do you know what I'm going to change it to?"

Earl's lips parted, as if he was actually going to take a guess, but then he compressed them again and gave just the smallest hint of a head shake to his employer.

"That makes two of us," Bennett said. "I don't know, either, but I'll think of something appropriate."

Bennett got up, went to the sideboard, and poured two brandies. He handed one to Earl and carried the other around his desk with him. He sat down and regarded his silent ally again.

"You know, Earl," he said, "this is going to sound funny—now, don't laugh!"

Earl didn't laugh.

"I consider you my closest friend. Isn't that funny?"

Earl still wasn't laughing.

"And to top it off, you're my closest friend," Bennett went on, "and I don't even remember if you *can* speak."

Earl seemed to be considering the remark, then raised his glass and sipped his brandy.

Gloria Bennett thought she heard voices coming from her husband's office. She hadn't heard anyone knock on the door, didn't think anyone but Cyrus was in the house—Cyrus and the cook.

At that moment, the black servant entered the foyer.

"Cyrus, do we have a visitor?"

"No, Ma'am," he said, "not that I know of.'

"I thought I heard my husband talking to someone."

"It must be Earl, Ma'am."

"Oh, all right. Thank you."

"Yes, Ma'am." Cyrus went on with whatever he was doing.

As far as Gloria knew, Earl had never said a word since his arrival several months ago. What kind of a conversation could her husband be having with such a man?

She sneaked down the hall and stopped only when she was able to make out her husband's words. It seemed obvious he was talking to himself, possibly using Earl as a sounding board. She listened for some time, her heart racing, and finally made her way back down the hall before she could be detected.

She had to get away and talk to Mike Casey fast!

Cyrus watched as Gloria Bennett left the house in a hurry, then walked down the hallway himself to his employer's office.

"Yes, Cyrus?" Bennett said, as he the black man appeared in the doorway.

"There's something you should know, sir."

"Tell me, then."

Cyrus looked at Earl, and then back at Bennett.

"It's all right, Cyrus," Bennett said. "You can talk in front of Earl."

"Yes, sir," Cyrus said. "I'm afraid Mrs. Bennett was listening at your door just now."

"Really?" Bennett said. "Hmmm. Heard me talking to Earl, did she?"

"Apparently so."

"Did she run out of here in a hurry?"

"A very big hurry, sir."

Bennett looked at Earl.

"Must be going to talk to her lover," he said. "It might

be time to make a serious move, Earl. What do you think?"

Cyrus didn't hear the big man reply, but Bennett acted as if he had. This worried Cyrus. It was as if his employer was hearing words that he could not.

"Thank you, Cyrus," Bennett said. "I appreciate the information."

"Yes, sir."

"Cyrus?" Bennett said, before the man could leave.

"Sir?"

"How long have you been with me?"

"For years, sir. I worked for your father, back east."

"Yes, so you did," Bennett said. "You're a very loyal man. I appreciate that."

"Thank you, sir."

"You can go."

"Yes, sir."

As Cyrus left, he heard Bennett say to Earl, "Okay, Earl, let's decide what to do."

TWENTY-SEVEN

Clint and Inga were watching the street from the window. Standing close together, Clint could smell her sweet scent but also his own sour one.

"Jesus, I need a bath," he said.

"We can do that," she said.

"How?"

She smiled.

"I'll give you a bath in bed."

"In bed?"

"Sure," she said, "we just need some soapy warm water and a cloth. If we're stuck in here, we might as well get you all clean and sweet smelling. Come on, you get in bed and I'll go get a basin and some cloths."

"Inga, I didn't mean—"

"Oh, come on," she said, "it will be fun."

"Dangerous" was more like it, but he walked to the bed and got in while she left the room to get the water.

All he had been wearing since he'd been shot was his own long underwear, and it was in need of washing. He had not been wearing it when he was shot, so it wasn't covered with blood. He had changed into it—or had been changed into it—later on.

Inga returned and said, "Take off your underwear."

"Take it off?"

She put the basin of warm, soapy water down on the table next to the bed and placed her hands on her hips.

"I can't bathe you while you're wearing it, and it needs to be washed, too. Come on, let me help you."

She reached for him but he said, "I can do it."

"Don't tell me you're shy all of a sudden?"

"No," Clint said, "I'm not shy."

He slid the long johns off his shoulders, got his arms out, and then needed her help to get them down over his legs. When he was naked, she soaked a cloth in water and began to wash him. She started with his feet and legs, cleaning them with an incredibly gentle touch, drying him before moving on to another part of his body.

She skirted his crotch, preferring to leave it for later, and began to clean his belly and chest. He couldn't help but respond to her touch, and his penis began to swell. She either didn't notice or, more than likely, was ignoring his condition.

"Roll onto your side. I need to clean your back."

He rolled over, and she gently bathed the area around his wounds and then did his buttocks and the back of his legs. If she wasn't becoming aroused by this—as he was—then she really would have made a great nurse.

"Okay," she said, "on your back, again. It doesn't hurt to lie on your back?"

"It's more discomfort than hurt."

"All right, then," she said. "One last area."

Her eyes went to his crotch. His penis was standing straight out, as hard as it had been in a long time.

"Inga—"

"Hush," she said, "I'm just washing you."

She rinsed the cloth, wrung it out, and then proceeded to clean the inside of his thighs and his testicles, lifting them gently to clean them thoroughly.

"Inga—" he said, tightly.

She ignored him. Using the cloth she wet his penis,

cleaning the head and then stroking the shaft—and then the cloth was gone and there was only her hand, stroking him up and down, up and down . . . and then she leaned over and took him into her mouth.

So much for being the perfect nurse.

"Jesus . . ." he said.

"Am I hurting you?" she asked, releasing him for a moment.

"Hell, no!"

She smiled, then opened her mouth and engulfed him again. She rode him up and down with her mouth, fondling his testicles at the same time. He groaned, sat up, and, leaning back on his hands, lifted his hips to the pressure of her mouth. He closed his eyes as he felt his release rushing up through his legs, and then suddenly he was exploding, spurting, again and again and again . . . and she sucked him until he had no more to give and he collapsed onto his back again, hissing as he came down too hard on one of his wounds.

"Well," she said, standing up, "I guess you're clean."

"You planned that, you wench," he said, later, when she had returned from putting away the basin.

"I did not," she said. "I was only trying to make you feel better by cleaning you."

"And?"

"And . . . I got carried away."

"You sure did."

"Don't you feel cleaner?"

"Oh, yes."

"And more relaxed."

"Definitely . . . but it's going to be awhile before I can walk again."

"Good," she said. "I want you to rest. I'll watch the window."

She walked to it, leaned against the wall and folded her arms.

"You know," she said, "when I found this town, I thought it would be a nice place to settle down."

"What changed your mind? All of this?"

"No," she said, "I think I changed my mind even before you came here. The people here are too desperate."

"For what?"

"Growth."

"And that's bad?"

She looked at him.

"I think being desperate for anything is bad," she said. "These people will do anything to try to have their town grow bigger."

"Including killing me?"

She looked at him and hugged herself as if she was cold.

"I knew you'd figure that out."

"It's quite a plan," Clint said. "Wait for someone with a reputation to ride in, kill them in some spectacular fashion, get your town on the map."

"I suppose."

"They didn't take into account one thing," Clint said.

"What's that?"

"My death would just as likely make this a ghost town as it would make it grow."

She looked at the floor.

"I guess they figured it was worth the chance."

"Who figured, Inga?" he asked. "Whose idea was it?"

"The council."

"Not Bennett?"

"Casey and Milburn were behind it more than anyone else," she said. "They just wanted to use Bennett's money. He moved here wanting to be accepted, and then wanting to take over. They made him think he was."

"So the town is using him?"

"His money."

"Do they think he's that dumb?"

"I don't know what they were thinking."

"Did you abstain from that vote, too, Inga?"

She didn't answer right away. He decided to wait and give her time to think about it.

"I didn't vote *against* it," she said, "but then I didn't know it would be you."

"You didn't know who it would be," he said. "What was the difference? Murder is murder."

"I told you this town is desperate," she said. "So was I. My business was not doing well, just like the others, and this was an idea that could have brought us some . . . attention, some business."

"And what do you think of the idea now?"

"I think it's awful," she said. "I thought it was awful when they first proposed it. And when they picked my place to shoot you, that's when I got mad." She looked at him imploringly. "You have to believe I didn't know they were going to do that. In fact, I was never sure they were really serious about the whole idea."

"I believe you."

"You do?"

"Yes."

"Why?"

"Because you didn't have to tell me any of this. Tell me, when this idea first came up, were you and Casey . . ."

"No," she said, "we were over before that."

"Inga," Clint said, "it's my experience that the more people who are involved in a conspiracy, the more likely there is to be trouble, people falling out with each other."

"I agree," she said. "That seems likely."

"I don't think Bennett is as dumb as the others think he is, and I think he's got a dangerous ally in that big fella, Earl. However, Mike Casey also strikes me as dangerous."

"He is."

"Apparently, he killed the five men who shot me. It doesn't matter to me if they were all together at the time, or if he killed them one at a time. Any man who can kill five men is dangerous."

"What do you intend to do?"

"Well," he said, "if I had the time, I'd like to just sit back and watch them go after each other. How close are the sheriff and the doctor?"

"Very close."

"Can the doctor use a gun?"

"Not that I know of."

"Then Casey had no backup."

"He has a part-time deputy, but he's just a store-keeper."

"So if Casey has to go up against Earl, and any other guns that Bennett might hire, he'll have to do it alone."

"He'll do it, too," she said. "He's not afraid."

"I need something I can use, Inga," Clint said. "Tell me what else you know about Casey."

"Well," she said, "I know the reason I stopped seeing him."

"Do you think that would be helpful?"

"Maybe."

"All right," he said, "what is it?"

TWENTY-EIGHT

Gloria looked for Mike Casey first at home and then at his office, where they had agreed she would never go.

"Gloria Bennett just went running into the sheriff's office," Inga told Clint. "That's not a smart thing to do."

"Wonder what that's all about?"

"I guess all we can do right now," Inga said, "is wonder."

When the office door slammed, Casey looked up and was surprised to see Gloria standing there.

"What are you doing here?" he asked. "You're not supposed to come here, Gloria."

"I had to," she said. "It's important."

"What is so important that you have to risk—"

"Brian knows about us."

"What?"

"I heard him telling Earl," she said.

"He was talking about it to Earl?" Casey frowned. "I didn't think Earl talked."

"Mike," she said, "what does it matter if Earl talks? Brian was talking *to* Earl *about* us."

"Okay, you're right," Casey said. "Tell me, what did he say?"

"That he knew we were sleeping together."

"And what else?"

"That he didn't care."

"Why not?"

"He said at least this way we were keeping each other occupied."

"Son of a bitch." Could it be, Casey thought, that Bennett actually was smarter than he and Milburn had figured?

"You have to kill him, Mike," she said, "you have to."

"Don't panic, Gloria," Casey said. "There's still a lot of things to be done here—"

"No," she said, grabbing his arm, "forget about Black Rock. We have to kill him and then go away together. There's plenty of money we can take with us. We can go to Europe!"

"What about the ranch?" Casey asked.

"Forget the ranch. He has a safe in the house that's filled with money."

"What about the money in the bank?"

"I can't get to that!" she said. "Only he can."

"Wait, wait," Casey said. "I've got to think. I've got to talk to Ed."

"Forget Ed, Mike," she said, putting her arms around his neck. "This is about you and me. He knows! What if he decides to send Earl after us?"

"I can handle Earl."

"What if Earl has help?"

"Gloria," he said, grabbing her arms, "you're panicking. Does he know that you know?"

"N-no," she said, "I don't—no, how could he?"

"All right, then," Casey said, "so as far as he knows, we're still keeping each other occupied. Look, I've been thinking about a few things. Sit down."

"I can't—"

"Sit down, relax, and listen to me," he said, leading her to a chair.

She sat down and tried to be calm. He crouched down in front of the chair and continued to hold her by the arms.

"I've been thinking," he said. "If our plan works for Black Rock, this could become an important place to live. I could become important because I'm the sheriff. The same goes for Ed because he's a doctor."

"I thought you didn't want to live in a big town or be sheriff of one?" she asked.

"I've changed my mind," he said. "I told you, I've been thinking about it. If we can put Black Rock on the map; it could be a place for you and me to live together."

"Together? What about Brian?"

"After we've succeeded with our plan, I'll do as you've been asking me," Casey said.

"Run away with me?"

"No," he said, "no, I mean . . . I'll kill him. I'll kill your husband."

She stared at him.

"After a respectable amount of time, you and I could get married and live on the ranch. I could continue to be sheriff. Our lives would change drastically, Gloria."

She bit her lips and studied his face.

"Of course," he said, "there's one thing we have to know before I can kill him."

"What's that?"

"We need to know if he leaves everything to you in his will. We need to know if there is a will."

"He does talk about a will, but I don't know if he leaves me everything."

"We have to find out," Casey said. "If there is a will and he doesn't leave everything to you, we'll have to get rid of it. If he dies without a will, you get everything."

"I understand," she said, "but what about . . . what about the fact that he knows about us?"

"Did he say that he was going to do anything about it?"

"Uh, n-no, he didn't."

"Then we have some time," Casey said. "He'll probably still want our plan to work before he does anything. All we have to do is wait until the Gunsmith gets back on his feet, kill him, and wait for everything to start going our way."

"But who's going to kill the Gunsmith?"

"Well," Casey said, "I guess if nobody else can do it, that job will fall to me. I'll kill Adams, then your husband, and then we can be together."

She stared at him and asked, "Can you do all that, Mike? Can you?"

"If you're with me on this, Gloria," he said, "I can do anything."

TWENTY-NINE

"She's out," Inga said.

"Where is she going?"

"She's just standing there, looking around. She doesn't seem as panicky as she did when she went in."

"Well, whatever was bothering her, apparently the sheriff was able to relax her."

Inga gave him a look.

"No, not like you relaxed me," he said. "She wasn't in there that long."

"She's walking away now."

"Keep watching," he said. "If she came in with a legitimate problem, then Casey is going to have to talk to Milburn about it."

"Why?"

"You said they were the brains behind the whole thing," Clint reminded her. "One probably doesn't make a move without the other. Look at how often they've both been up here to see me."

"Do you think either one of them has noticed yet that I've locked up?" she asked.

"Probably not," he said, "but they will. Did he come out yet?"

"No."

"Then he's not panicked by what she had to say."

"Clint," she said, "I've been thinking about something."

"What?"

"What if we just left?"

"You don't want to leave everything you own."

"Well, what if I did?"

"We can't do that."

"Why not?"

"I can't ride."

"I'll get a buckboard," she said. "We'll sneak out the back at night and be gone before anyone even notices."

"It's a thought," Clint said, "but I don't think it would work."

"Why not?"

"Well, first you'd have to get my horse from the livery," he said. "Second, you'd have to get two more horses and a buckboard. I don't think you could do that without the sheriff finding out. I mean, look what happened with the telegraph clerk."

"We're still not sure he told Mike anything."

"Maybe not," Clint said, "but it sure seems likely."

Inga started to say something, but the door to the sheriff's office opened at that moment.

"He's coming out."

"Does he looked agitated?"

"No," she said, "he appears very calm. He's walking in the direction of the doctor's office."

"What else is that way?"

"The saloon and the telegraph office, among other things."

"Can you see the doctor's office from here?

"No," she said. "I'd have to open the window and stick my head out."

"Never mind. Inga, is there anyone in this town you trust?"

She thought a moment, then said, "No."

"There's no one you consider a friend?"

"I did not make friends very easily when I came here," she said. "Men were crude to me, and women didn't like me. They still don't."

"Beautiful women have that problem, I guess."

"It is not worth being beautiful to have to deal with them." She walked away from the window and sat on the edge of the bed. "Do you still think help will come?"

"There won't be a lot of it," he said, "but someone will come. I guess how much help they are will depend on who it is."

"Well," she said, "I hope it's soon."

Bat Masterson wondered why things like this always happened when you were in a hurry. He couldn't remember the last time a horse he was riding stepped into a chuckhole. Mounted, he was a day away from Black Rock. Walking, leading a lame horse as he was now, who knew how long it would take him to get there?

THIRTY

Dave Manners had only been Brian Bennett's foreman
for the past year. The only duties he'd had in all that
time dealt with the ranch. Most of his orders came in
the morning, with Bennett standing on the porch of his
house and the foreman in front of the house. That's why
Manners was surprised to be invited into the house on
this day. Not only was he invited into the house, but into
his boss's den and handed a glass of brandy.

"Dave," Bennett said, "did you ever wonder why I
hired you to be my foreman when you had no experience?"

"No, sir."

"You didn't."

"I mean, yes, sir."

Manners was a bit nervous, especially with the big
man, Earl, standing behind him.

Bennett smiled. He knew he had not hired Manners
for his brains, so the man's reactions did not bother him.

"I'm going to tell you why I hired you," Bennett said.
"First, you're an ugly man."

Manners touched his face. Women had told him that
before, so this came as no surprise, and it did nothing
to hurt his feelings.

"That wasn't a problem because, as you can see, I'm rather ugly, myself. So that worked in your favor."

Manners didn't know what to say, so he said, "Yes, sir," again.

"Secondly," Bennett said, "I did a thorough check of your background."

Uh-oh, Manners thought, *here it comes*. He'd been waiting a year for this to happen.

"I know about your prison record."

Manners put down the brandy glass and started to rise.

"I'll pack my gear—"

"No, no," Bennett said, "don't be silly. Sit back down."

"I'm not fired?"

"Not at all."

Manners sat back down and stared across the desk at his boss.

"I'm telling you that I knew all of this about you when I hired you. Come on, pick up your glass."

Manners obeyed, but he didn't drink. He preferred rotgut whiskey to this fancy stuff.

"Now, the reason I hired you even though I knew about your record is that I thought someday I'd be able to use you."

"To do what?" Manners asked.

"Why were you in jail?"

Manners looked around nervously. He was forty-five and, truth be told, he had spent half his life in jail. He was sure, though, that his boss was talking about the last time he was in jail.

"You killed a woman, didn't you?"

"Yes, sir," Manners said. "A man and a woman."

"And why did you kill them?"

"The woman was my wife," he said, "and I caught them together."

"And you went into a rage and killed them."

"Yes, sir."

"And served your time for it."

"Yes, sir."

"Fifteen years?"

"Yes, sir." Manners was surprised that Bennett seemed to know just about everything.

"And you came out about the time I hired you, right?"

"Yes, sir."

"Have you liked working here?"

"Yes, sir, I have."

"I can tell," Bennett said. "You do a good job."

"Thank you, sir."

"And the men seem to respect you."

"I think they do."

"Do you want to keep on working here?"

"Yes, sir, I do."

"A lot?"

"A whole lot."

"And what would you do to keep working here?"

"Mr. Bennett," Manners said, "I think I would do just about anything to keep my job, sir. Anything."

"That's what I wanted to hear, Dave. Why don't you hand that brandy to Earl, there. Earl, get rid of that for Dave and get him a real glass of whiskey. Dave, we have some business to discuss."

THIRTY-ONE

"What are you doing?" Inga demanded as Clint swung his feet to the floor.

"I need to get dressed."

She hurried to his side and tried to push him back into bed. He fended her off.

"Inga, I need your help."

"I'm trying to help you."

"No, I need your help in getting dressed."

"So you can do what?"

"Things I can't do while I'm in bed," Clint said. "Look, the time has come to do something other than lying around and waiting."

"Your wounds are going to open."

"That's why I need your help," he said. "I want you to dress them freshly and then bind me up like I had broken ribs. Just wrap tape around me so that the wounds are tightly bound. You got that?"

"And what will that do?"

"I hope it will keep me from bleeding to death."

"While you do what?"

"Probably what I should have been doing all along," he said. "Stirring the pot a little."

•   •   •

"How do you feel?"

"I can barely breathe," he said.

"I probably wrapped you too tight," she said. "I can loosen—"

"No, no," he said, "it's fine, really."

He walked across the room, enjoying the feel of being dressed again and having his boots on. He picked up his gunbelt, strapped it on, and that's when he really felt better.

"Do you have a back door?"

"Yes. What are you going to do?"

"I just want to have a look around town, first," Clint said, "and see what I'm up against." In reality, he just wanted to move around and see how he felt. There wasn't going to be much for him to see. For the things he really wanted to do he had to test his body, and that's what this little nighttime turn around town was supposed to do.

He walked to the window and looked out. It was just starting to get dark, and the streets were not busy at all, as most of the businesses were closing for the day. From down the street he could hear music, as the saloon was actually gearing up for the night.

"All right," he said. "Take me down to the back door."

They left the room, and he followed her down the hall and down the stairs. When they got to the back door she unlocked it with a key.

"Let me have the key," he said. "I'll lock it behind me, and you won't have to worry about letting me in."

She gave him the key, and he closed his left hand over it. The wound on his upper arm was tightly bound, as were the others, and he was glad he had managed to avoid taking a bullet in his right arm, because that was the one he was going to be needing.

"Clint," she said, "be careful."

"Don't worry," he said. "Getting shot four times tends to make a man more careful than ever before."

THIRTY-TWO

After Clint slipped out the back door and locked it behind him, he made his way along the back of Inga's building to the alley that ran alongside it. He decided the best way to be spotted on the streets was to be skulking along. He decided to simply walk, although he would make a point of keeping to the shadows. He didn't want anyone recognizing him and possibly taking a shot at him. If the doctor or the sheriff recognized him—well, he'd just have to say that he sneaked out for a walk to test himself, and see where that got him.

His movements were stiff, restricted by the bandages that wound around his chest and waist. They itched and were uncomfortable, but they would do the job and keep him from bleeding—at least he hoped they would.

He had told Inga he wanted to take a look around, but he had seen all he had to see of Black Rock his first day there. He decided to go to the livery to check up on Duke, and let the big gelding know that he hadn't forgotten about him.

When he reached the livery, the front doors were closed. There was a side door, however, and when he tried it, it opened. He stepped inside and found himself in the dark. He groped the walls on either side of the

125

door and found a storm lamp hanging on one side. He fished a lucifer from his pocket, struck it, and lit the wick on the lamp. It was about a quarter filled with oil, enough for his task.

He carried the lamp to Duke's stall and hung it on a nail. He entered the stall and touched Duke's massive neck and spoke to him.

"How you doing, big boy?"

Duke's head came around, and the animal looked right at him.

"Bet you been wondering where I've been, huh?"

Duke looked bored, but Clint chose to believe that the look was contrived. The big gelding just didn't want him to know how much he cared.

He ran his hands along the horse's back, up and down his legs, checking his condition.

"Somebody's been taking good care of you," he said, "but I bet you could use some exercise, huh? So could I. In fact, I'm tempted just to saddle you up now and get the hell out of here. Wouldn't that be something? If we left here and just disappeared? Only where could we go to do that? Bolivia? It's been tried. No, we'll have to do what we always do, see the hand through."

Clint checked Duke's feed bin and saw that he had more than enough food.

"Okay, fella, I've got to go," Clint said. "I just wanted to make sure you knew I was still alive."

He walked to the horse's head and ran his hand along Duke's nose. The big gelding finally gave in and nudged Clint in the chest, saying hello.

"There you go," Clint said, rubbing Duke's nose with great affection. "I knew you couldn't carry off that aloof act forever."

Insulted, Duke reclaimed his nose and stuck it in the feed bin, pointedly ignoring Clint.

"Okay," Clint said, "have it your way. I'll be back soon, and we'll go out and get some exercise."

Clint looked around and made sure his saddle was still in the livery. His rifle was in Inga's building somewhere. When he got back, he'd have to ask her for it.

He took the lamp from the nail and carried it back to the side door. He hung it back up and then turned the flame down until it was doused. That done, he opened the door and stepped outside. One thing was off his mind. Satisfied that Duke was all right, he could move on to other things.

Like staying alive.

He took a turn around town, just for the exercise, and stopped just outside the saloon. He peered in the front window. At a table he saw Sheriff Casey sitting with Doctor Ed Milburn. Both men had mugs of beer and appeared to be staring into them morosely. *Sorry boys*, he thought, *things just aren't going as planned, are they?*

The doctor looked up and Clint ducked back to hopefully avoid being seen. It was time to get back to Inga's. He'd had enough exercise for one night.

THIRTY-THREE

"What is it?" Casey asked.

Milburn wiped his hand over his eyes.

"I think I had too much to drink."

"Why?"

Milburn pointed.

"I thought I saw Clint Adams's face looking in the front window of the saloon."

Casey turned around to look, and saw nothing.

"What are you talkin' about? I don't see anything."

"He's gone now."

"He's flat on his back, Ed."

"I know it," Milburn said. "I told you, I probably had too much to drink."

"Would it be possible for him to get up?" Casey asked.

"Anything's possible, I suppose," Milburn said, "but those wounds should keep him in bed for another week."

Casey stood up.

"I'm going to have a look around. Wait here."

"I'll come with—"

"Just wait here!"

Milburn sank back onto his seat as Mike Casey headed for the saloon doors.

•   •   •

When Clint unlocked the back door of Inga's building
and entered, he was out of breath. If Milburn had seen
him in the window, he'd mention it to Casey. The sheriff
would probably come out and have a look. To avoid
being seen, Clint hightailed it back and exerted himself
more than he had planned.

He got inside, and suddenly his legs turned to jelly.
He locked the door, then slid down into a seated position
on the floor, his back against the door. Moments later,
Inga came down the hall with a lamp.

"Jesus," she said, "what happened?"

"I'm just . . . a little out of . . . breath," Clint said.

"Can you get up?"

Clint made an effort, then said, "Not right now. Just
let me sit here a minute."

Inga put the lamp on the floor. She was still dressed,
preferring to stay that way while waiting for him to
come back. She sat on the floor next to him.

"What happened?"

"I took a look into the saloon," Clint said. "I think
the doctor saw my face in the window."

"Oh, God!"

"I got back here before anyone could see me," Clint
said. "He'll think he imagined it."

"Was he with Mike?"

"Yes."

"What if they're on their way here to check?"

He looked at her.

"That's possible, I suppose."

"We have to get you back to bed." She got to her feet,
picked the lamp up from the floor. "Come on. You can
lean on me."

She reached one hand down to help him to his feet,
and then he did lean on her. She staggered a bit, almost
dropping the lamp, but then righted herself and took his
weight. Together they walked down the hall until they

reached the staircase. There he transferred his weight to the bannister, and she simply guided him up. He seemed to regain some of the strength in his legs so that he was able to walk to the room from the stairs, but when they got there, he quickly collapsed on the bed and passed out.

Mike Casey stepped out in front of the saloon and looked both ways. There was no sign of Clint Adams, or anyone. He couldn't even hear anyone. Maybe Milburn was right. Maybe he'd had too much to drink, like he said. He was about to go inside when he decided to go to Inga's and double-check, just to make sure Adams was still in bed.

"I told you." Clint heard Inga's voice as if it was coming from a tunnel. "Are you satisfied?"

He opened his eyes and saw two faces floating above him.

"Adams? Are you awake?"

Slowly, the face of the man speaking came into view, and it was Mike Casey's.

"Sheriff?" Clint said. "Is there a problem?"

"No, no," Casey said, "nothing. I just wanted to check and see if you were all right."

"I am all right," Clint said. "In fact, I was asleep."

"I told him that," Inga said.

"I'm sorry," Casey said. "I'll, uh, let you get back to sleep. I'll check on you tomorrow."

"Fine. Good night."

"Uh, good night."

Inga hustled the sheriff to the door of the room and said, "Let yourself out. I'll lock up later."

She closed the door behind the lawman and then hurried to the bed.

"Are you all right?"

"What happened?"

"You fainted," she said. "I just barely got you into bed when the sheriff started banging on the door. I didn't even have time to undress you."

Clint looked down, grabbed the covers and lifted them to see that he was still fully dressed—boots and all. He was lucky the sheriff hadn't decided to take a look.

"Jesus," Clint said. "The doctor must have seen me after all. Good thing you're a quick thinker."

"Let me help you get undressed."

"Go downstairs and lock up. I can undress myself. Go on."

As she left to lock up, he swung his feet to the floor and began to undress. The next thing he knew, Inga was waking him up again.

"You fainted," she said.

"Again?"

"Come on," she said, and helped him with the rest of his clothes. When he was down to his shorts, she pushed him down on the bed and covered him.

"I knew you shouldn't have gone out," she said. She touched his face. "You're even feverish."

"I'll be okay," he told her. "I just need to rest a little."

"That's just what I've been telling you."

"I mean just for tonight. Tell me, what did the sheriff say when he came over?"

"Just that he wanted to check on you. I told him you were sleeping, but he insisted."

"You were smart to let him up."

"You looked awful when you woke up," she said, "so pale."

"Good," Clint said. "Maybe now he'll be convinced that the doctor was seeing things."

"You better close your eyes, now," she said.

"What are you going to do?" he asked, sleepily.

"I'm going to watch over you."

"Good," he said, his eyes closing, "only could you do it quietly. . . ?"

THIRTY-FOUR

Big Earl was Brian Bennett's most obvious weapon. Dave Manners, on the other hand, was his secret weapon. Bennett felt that by putting the two together he had the advantage over Mike Casey, and Clint Adams.

Bennett decided that both Casey and Adams had to die. He knew more than Casey and Milburn thought he knew. For instance, he knew that they thought he was stupid, a rich buffoon who thought with his money and not with his brain. But they were wrong. They were all wrong about him, just as everyone was wrong about him when he was growing up. He wasn't just a short, ugly, gnomish little man, and he was going to prove it.

Once Casey was dead, Milburn and the rest of the town would fall into line.

Clint Adams was another matter. Bennett could tell by looking at the man, and talking to him, that he—like himself—was acting for the sake of the sheriff and the doctor. Brian Bennett had spent most of his life acting—acting as though the constant ridicule heaped on him by his peers didn't bother him; acting as if the revolted looks he received from his own family didn't affect him. It was all this acting that enabled him to see it in other people, like Gloria, who acted as if she loved him; like

Mike Casey, who acted as if he wasn't sleeping with
Gloria; like Doc Milburn, who acted like he thought
Brian Bennett was important; and like Clint Adams,
who, he was sure, was acting as if he was more injured
than he actually was.

Granted, the man had been shot four times, but ac-
cording to Doc Milburn, none of the wounds in and of
themselves was life threatening—and he was sure that a
man like the Gunsmith had been shot before.

The only thing he needed to figure out was the order
in which these people were to be eliminated: Gloria,
Mike Casey, and Clint Adams. They were all a threat to
him and all had to go.

Now, who first?

Gloria decided not to go back to her husband's house,
but to wait for Mike Casey at his house on the edge of
town. All this time she thought that she and her lover
were pulling the wool over Brian's eyes, and all this
time he'd known what was going on. Suddenly, the little
man she was married to wasn't an ugly joke, but something to fear. She decided that nothing was worth going
back to him, not his ranch or his money. She had to
make Casey realize that nothing was important but the
two of them.

She was sitting, curled up on Casey's couch, when
she heard a door open. She couldn't tell if it was the
front door, or the back.

"Mike?"

She remained curled in a ball on the sofa, hugging a
cushion to her, listening intently.

"Is that you, Mike?"

Suddenly, a man entered the room, a large man who
was not Mike Casey, but a man she knew from the
ranch. She'd never exchanged any words with him, but
this was the man her husband had hired to be his foreman some time back.

"What . . . what do you want?"

The man advanced on her. He held no weapon, but he had big hands, which at that moment were curled and menacing.

"I'm sorry, Ma'am," the man said, "this is nothing personal."

And the hands reached toward her. . . .

When Mike Casey left Inga's apothecary shop, he looked up at the window of the room Clint Adams was in. Casey had made it a rule never to underestimate an adversary—especially one the caliber of Clint Adams—and yet he thought he had. Adams, he decided, was much more dangerous, even in his present condition, than he had imagined. It had been obvious to him that the man, although lying in bed, had been wearing boots. It was also likely that he had been dressed beneath the bedclothes. Doc Milburn had been right. He had seen Clint Adams outside the saloon. Adams had been playing possum all this time and was much further along in his recovery than even the doctor thought.

Casey was momentarily unable to decide what to do. It was as if his mind had frozen up. First Gloria tells him that her husband knows about them, and now this. Who was the more immediate threat to him, Bennett or Adams? Physically, Adams was. Even in his present condition he posed a more physical threat than the diminutive Bennett. However, Bennett had Earl—and who knew who else—backing his play, while Adams only seemed to have Inga. This made Bennett the most immediate threat.

It was too late to do anything about it now, but in the morning he'd talk to Milburn. They could no longer feel that they were controlling Brian Bennett. The man was not the fool they had thought he was. He and the doc were going to have to come up with a plan to get out of this. Maybe the most likely one was to just get away.

Leave the town to Bennett, get away from the Gunsmith, even take Gloria with him.

He walked to his house on the edge of town and as he approached the front door saw that it was wide open. He had told Gloria to go back home, but it seemed that she'd had other plans. Why, though, had she left the door open? So that her presence wouldn't startle him?

He entered the house and called her name. When there was no answer, he drew his gun.

"Gloria?" he called again.

Still no reply.

He moved forward slowly, gun extended, until he was in the living room. A lamp next to the sofa was lit. He could see a woman on the sofa, so it was apparent that she was lying there. Had she fallen asleep waiting for him?

"Gloria," he said, "come on, wake up. I thought I told you—"

He'd been moving towards her as he spoke and stopped short when her face and head came into view. Her head was twisted at an unnatural angle, and her eyes were wide open and sightless.

"Shit," he swore, softly.

It was too late to get out.

THIRTY-FIVE

The next morning Mike Casey and Doc Milburn were sitting in his office having coffee. Milburn was looking worn out and disheveled.

"I can't believe I did what I did last night," he said.

"It had to be done, Ed."

"But to bury her like that, with no marker?"

"I couldn't have her found dead in my house," Casey said. "How would that have looked?"

"We could have moved the body somewhere else."

"No," Casey said, "people would still be looking at me to solve her murder, and we don't have time for that."

"Are you sure Bennett had her killed?"

"Who else would do it?" Casey asked.

"Maybe she was sleeping with someone, and he killed her out of jealousy," Milburn said.

"Ed, I was the only one she was sleeping with."

Milburn looked at him.

"I didn't kill her, Ed."

"I know you didn't, Mike," the doctor said, "but for somebody who was in love with her, you don't look all broken up about her death."

"Who said I was in love with her?" Casey asked.

137

"You weren't?"

"I was just sleeping with her."

"I thought—"

"You thought wrong."

"Still," Milburn said, "if I had been sleeping with her, I don't think I could have just stuck her in a hole in the ground."

"You better stop thinking about her," Casey said, "and start thinking about Bennett. If Bennett had his own wife killed, what do you think he has planned for the two of us?"

"It must have been that Earl."

"I don't care who actually did it," Casey said. "Whoever it was works for Bennett, and he's the one we have to worry about."

"Do you think he knows what we've been planning?"

"I don't think he's anywhere near as dumb as we've been thinking he is," Casey said. "This was his way of showing it."

Milburn got up and poured himself another cup of coffee. He noticed that his fingernails were caked with dirt.

"What's he gonna do when her body isn't found today?" he asked.

"I don't know," Casey said. "I just wanted to have some extra time to decide what we're going to do."

"And what's that?"

"I'm still trying to decide."

"What if we go to him and offer him an equal partnership?"

"What's he need us for?" Casey asked. "He's got the money, and he can hire someone to kill Adams for him."

"But . . . we have the town council behind us."

"Not if we're dead, we don't."

Casey poured himself some more coffee and took it behind his desk.

"Why would he kill me?" Milburn asked. "I'm no threat to him, not the way you are."

"Me?"

"Sure, you're the sheriff. You're good with a gun," Milburn said. "You're the threat to him."

"I don't like what I'm hearing, Ed," Casey said, sitting forward. "We're in this together, you know. We conceived this idea together the day Adams got to town."

"We should have laid our cards on the table to Bennett that day instead of trying to figure out a way to use him."

"It's too late for that kind of thinking now," Casey said, "but you are right about one thing."

"And what's that?"

"If he's going to kill one of us, it's going to be me," Casey said. "You and the rest of the council would fall in line after that."

Milburn didn't argue. In fact, he said, "I hate to say it, but I think you're right about that. You better be real careful, Mike. Is there anyone in town you can count on to back you up?"

"What about you?"

"Me?" Milburn said, sounding shocked. "I've never shot anyone in my life. What about your deputy?"

"Part-time deputy, you mean," Casey said. "I think Sam Morgan is in the same situation you are, Ed."

"Well then, who can you use?"

"There's only one man in town I'd count on to keep me alive," Casey said, thoughtfully.

"Yeah? Who would that be?"

Mike Casey didn't reply, because he thought the answer was quite obvious.

THIRTY-SIX

When Clint woke the next morning, the night before was a little foggy. Inga entered with his breakfast and filled him in on what had happened after he returned.

"You kept fainting," she said. "You pushed yourself too far."

"Was the sheriff here?"

"Yes," Inga said. "Doctor Milburn said he thought he saw you outside the saloon. Mike came here to check. I had to throw the covers over you while you were still dressed."

"I remember now," he said. "That wouldn't have fooled the sheriff. He's too sharp."

"You're saying he knows you were outside?"

"Probably."

"Then he knows you've been on your feet. What he doesn't know is that it took a lot out of you."

"Actually," Clint said, "I feel pretty good, this morning—and I'm hungry."

He attacked the meal she had brought him—bacon, eggs, and rolls, with hot coffee.

"What do we do today, then?" she asked.

"I'll have to get up to see if last night really took something out of me," he said.

"First I have to unwrap you to see if you did your wounds any harm," she said.

"Fine," he said, "but I don't think I did. You did a really good job last night."

Suddenly, there was the sound of someone knocking downstairs.

"I'll see who it is," Inga said.

"Don't open it unless you know them."

She nodded and went downstairs. When she got there, she saw Mike Casey peering in the window.

"Open up, Inga," he said. "I have to talk to Adams."

"What about?"

"Something that will benefit him and me," he said. "Come on, open the door."

She hesitated, then unlocked the door and let him in.

"Why are you all locked up?"

"For safety."

"Can't blame you for that. Is he awake?"

"He's eating breakfast."

"I'll take some coffee, if you have it."

"He has a pot," she said. "I'll bring in an extra cup."

"Thanks."

"What's this about, Mike?"

"Survival."

He went upstairs and entered the room.

" 'Morning, Adams," he said. "Are you recovered from your night out last night?"

"I told Inga you wouldn't be fooled. What was it? The boots?"

"Hard to hide boots under the covers," Casey said.

Inga came in with another cup.

"Do you mind sharing your coffee?" she asked Clint.

"Not at all," Clint said.

Inga poured Casey a cup. The sheriff took a sip and eyed Clint's bandages.

"Looks like you were wrapped up pretty tightly."

"Inga's a good nurse."

Inga stared at Clint.

"The sheriff knows I was out last night, Inga. Don't worry about it."

"I want to see if you made yourself bleed." She looked at Casey. "Can I do that while you talk?"

"Sure, why not?"

Clint sat up and Inga carefully unwrapped him.

"I suppose we're both going to put our cards on the table," Clint said.

"I am," Casey said. "I need your help."

"You were in on a conspiracy to kill me, and now you want my help?" Clint asked.

"That's it exactly."

"Well, you've got balls, I'll give you that," Clint said. "Go ahead, explain yourself."

Casey looked at Inga, wondering if he should make her leave the room.

"I'm not going anywhere," she said, as if reading his mind, "so you might as well say what you want to say, Mike."

"All right," Casey said. "Gloria Bennett is dead."

Inga gasped.

"How?" Clint asked.

"Somebody broke her neck."

"Where did it happen?"

"In my house," Casey said. "I found her there last night after I left here."

"And what did you do?"

Casey looked away and said, "I buried her."

"Mike!"

"I can't afford to have it known she was in my house, Inga," Casey said. He looked at Clint. "You understand, don't you?"

"I understand how you'd think that," Clint said. "I don't understand how you could do it."

"Self-preservation kicked in, I guess."

"Did the doctor help?" Clint asked.

"Yes."

"He must be feeling guilty," Clint said. "Goes against his oath."

"He's a good friend."

"He'd have to be. What do you want from me, Sheriff?"

"Gloria's death was a message from Brian Bennett," Casey said. "He's going to come after me next."

"Wait just a minute," Clint said. "You're not about to ask me to watch your back, are you?"

"Of all the nerve," Inga said.

"That's what I'm asking," Mike Casey said.

Clint stared at him, shook his head and then said, "Yeah, you do have balls, Sheriff."

THIRTY-SEVEN

"How can he help you when he can't get out of bed?" Inga demanded.

"He was out of bed last night," Casey pointed out.

"And it almost killed him!"

Casey looked at Clint.

"She's exaggerating," he said, "but it did take something out of me."

"He collapsed when he came back," she said, "and he had a fever."

"No fever today, though," Clint said.

Inga glared at him.

"You're actually going to help him?"

"I didn't say that."

"Yet," Casey said.

"Tell me why I should?" Clint asked.

"I know I have no right to ask, but after Bennett gets rid of me," Casey said, "you'll be next on his list."

"Do you think his man Earl killed his wife?"

"He's sure big and strong enough to have done it."

"He wears a shoulder rig like he knows how," Clint said. "Just because he's a big, strong man doesn't mean he kills with his hands."

"Bennett has a lot of men working for him."

"Killers? Or ranch hands?"

Casey shrugged.

"Who knows?"

Inga finished examining Clint's wounds. Remarkably, none of them had bled the night before.

"Wrap me up again, Inga," Clint said.

"You'll help me?" Casey asked.

"I haven't decided yet, Sheriff."

"Well," Casey said, "think it over. I don't know how much time we have left, but I suppose it can wait a day. Bennett might wait to hear about his wife being found."

"But she won't, will she?" Inga asked. "You just dumped her in a hole in the ground."

"I'm not proud of what I did, Inga," Casey said. He looked at Clint. "I'm not proud of any of it. I got caught up in it, like everyone else." He looked at Inga again. "When this is all over with, I'll dig her up again and give her a proper burial. I promise."

Clint looked at the lawman and said, pointedly, "That is, if you don't get one first."

"Yeah," Sheriff Mike Casey said, "there is that."

THIRTY-EIGHT

That morning, Dave Manners was once again in front of Brian Bennett's desk.

"I assume you had no problem last night?" Bennett asked.

"None."

"Good, good. Now I need a man to go into town and wait around until the news breaks. Do you have someone you can trust to send?"

"Yes, sir."

"And what about when push comes to shove, Dave?" Bennett asked. "Do we have any men who will stand with us?"

"Well, I got sort of a confession to make, Mr. Bennett."

"And what's that, Dave?"

"When you made me foreman and gave me the power to hire, I, uh, sort of hired some, uh, old friends."

"Old friends?"

"Cellmates, sir."

"So there are other men working here who are like you?" Bennett asked. "I mean, they have a checkered past?"

"Yes, sir."

"Well, that's very good news, Dave," Bennett said, "Very good news, indeed."

"It is?"

"I'm going to need some men who can get the job done, men like yourself. How many of these, uh, friends are there?"

"Three."

Bennett smiled.

"A good number," he said. "Yes, that will work. With you, and them, and Earl . . . yes, I do believe this is going to work just fine. Dave, get your men together. Pick one out to go to town and have the rest stand by. I'll want them—and you—ready at a moment's notice."

"Whatever you say, Boss."

In point of fact, Dave Manners enjoyed what he had done last night—that is, after the initial wave of sadness at having to kill so pretty a woman. But being a ranch foreman had started to wear thin on him, just as being ranch hands had started wearing thin on his friends. This was going to be the kind of work they all preferred.

"I'll get right on it."

"You do that, Dave."

Manners turned to leave, but caught himself short when he saw Earl in the doorway. They matched looks for a few moments, and then Earl stepped aside to let the foreman out.

"Dave is tuning out to be quite a surprise," Bennett said to Earl. "Quite a surprise."

THIRTY-NINE

"You can't be serious," Inga said.

"Why not?" he asked. "Weren't you in on this scheme early on?"

"That's different," she said. "The whole thing was his idea."

"I'm not saying I'm going to forgive him for anything," Clint said.

"But you'll trust him to watch your back?"

"As long as I'm watching his," Clint said, "he'll be watching mine."

"Didn't you say something about stirring the pot?" she asked.

"And I still intend to."

"How?"

"I'll have a talk with Bennett."

"You're going to go out to his ranch?"

"I don't know," Clint said, "I haven't decided."

"Are you going to double-cross Mike?"

"I'll keep him alive as long as he keeps me alive. I just want to give Bennett something to think about. Right now he seems to have all the cards. I need to find myself a wild one."

"Where will you find that?"

"I don't know," Clint said, "maybe it will just come riding into town."

At that moment, Bat Masterson reined in his new horse at the sign that proclaimed the city limits of Black Rock. It had taken him a while to walk his lame horse to a town where he could find a new one. He'd had to trade the lame horse, which, once it healed up, would be better than the nag he was riding now. He hoped that Clint would appreciate that he'd given up a good piece of horseflesh to get here to help him.

That is, if Clint was still alive.

Gunther Morgan rode into town from the opposite direction as Bat Masterson, having come from the Bennett ranch. Gunther had served five years with Dave Manners, and when Manners got the job working for Bennett, he sent for Gunther. They had agreed that whoever got a job would try to help the other one. Gunther appreciated the job Manners had gotten him, but did not appreciate being a ranch hand. This was much more to his liking.

He left his horse at the livery, found the apothecary shop, and took up position across from it. Armed with Clint Adams's description, he settled down to watch.

Masterson rode up to the hotel, the only one that Black Rock seemed to have, and tied his horse outside. He went inside and approached the clerk at the front desk.

"Can I get you a room?" the man asked.

"That depends," Masterson said. "Is Clint Adams registered here?"

"Why yes, Mr. Adams is registered," the man said, "sort of."

"What do you mean, sort of?"

"Well . . . there was an incident a couple of weeks or so ago, and he was shot. He was staying here at the

time, but I understand he's recovering in a room above
the apothecary shop."

"Apothecary?"

"Shop," the man said, nodding. "See, that's where he
was shot."

"Apothecary shop."

"Yes."

"And where's that?"

The clerk gave him directions, telling him it was just
down the street and that he couldn't miss it.

"So then I guess Adams is still alive?"

"Last I heard," the man said. "We all thought he was
gonna die, but it looks like he pulled through. Heard he
was shot four times."

Bat winced.

"All right, then," Bat said, "I suppose now you might
as well give me a room."

"You a friend of Clint Adams?" the man asked.

Bat hesitated before answering, then said noncom-
mittally, "I know who he is and heard something about
him being here. I was just curious."

FORTY

Even though she had closed the shop, Inga still went downstairs to do some work. She was behind the counter when someone knocked on the door. She thought it was going to be the sheriff and was ready to yell at him, but when she looked up she saw a handsome man in his early thirties peering in the window. She walked to the door and opened it. There was something about the man that told her he was no threat.

"Can I help you?"

The man looked her up and down appreciatively and said, "Now I understand why Clint is recuperating here."

"Excuse me?"

"He is here, isn't he?" Bat Masterson asked. "Clint Adams?"

"Why do you want to know?"

Suddenly the man smiled and said, "You're Inga, aren't you?"

"Well, yes, but, how . . ."

He took her telegram from his pocket and held it out. "You sent this?"

"Why, yes. Are you . . . Mister Hartman?"

"No," he said, "but Rick Hartman sent me. I'm here to help Clint. Now, is he here?"

"Yes, he's upstairs."

"Would you like to go up and tell him a friend of his is here?"

She studied him for a moment and got the same feeling that had made her open the door.

"No," she said, "that's all right. I will take you up."

"What kind of accent is that, if you don't mind me asking?" he said as he entered.

"Swedish," she said, touching her mouth. "I thought it was gone."

"No," he said, "it's not quite gone—and I hope it never is. It's charming, utterly charming."

She closed the door, feeling flushed and warm, then turned to him and said, "Follow me, please."

Gunther saw the man walk to the apothecary shop and knock on the door. He didn't know what "apothecary" meant, and he didn't know where the man had come from. He watched as a pretty woman opened the door and talked to the man for a while, and then she let him in. He didn't know what to do after that, so he just waited.

Upstairs, Inga knocked on the door and opened it enough to stick her head in. Clint looked at her from the bed, where he was sitting, fully clothed, rather then lying under the covers.

"A friend of yours is here," she said and opened the door wider.

Clint started reaching for the gun on the bedpost, but stopped when Bat Masterson stepped into the room, followed by Inga.

"Well," Bat said, "you look pretty damn good for a man who was shot four times."

"Well, I'll be—" Clint said. "Inga, meet my wild card, Bat Masterson."

While Clint filled Bat in on the events of the past couple of weeks, Inga went to make coffee. By the time she returned, Bat Masterson had all the facts at his disposal.

"So you think there's a falling out among these, uh, murderers, huh?" Bat asked. "The sheriff wants to get Bennett before Bennett can get the sheriff?"

"Something like that," Clint said. "I don't think the sheriff expects me to help him kill Bennett, but he sure wants me to help keep him alive."

"Well," Bat said, accepting a cup of coffee from Inga, "I wonder which of them is responsible for the man in the doorway across the street?"

FORTY-ONE

"Inga," Clint said, "go to the window and have a look. Try not to be too obvious."

She did as she was told and looked at the man in the doorway.

"Do you know him?"

"No."

"He's not from town?"

She hesitated, then said, "I don't think so."

Clint looked at Bat.

"He must be one of Bennett's men."

"What can you tell me about Bennett?" Bat asked.

"A rich man, trying to make up for lack of height and looks with money," Clint said.

"What else is new? You know, all in all this wasn't a bad plan."

"What?" Inga asked.

Bat looked at her.

"Granted, it could have gone either way. This town could have grown with the curiosity factor, or died because of it, but still, the people decided to do something for themselves."

"Is he serious?" Inga asked Clint.

"He admires ingenuity," Clint said.

"But they tried to kill you."

"I know they tried to kill him," Bat assured her, "and I'm here to make sure he gets out of Black Rock alive."

"Just the two of you?"

"Hey," Clint said, "my chances are twice as good as they were yesterday. I'll take that any day."

"Besides," Bat said, "the sheriff's on our side, too, isn't he?" He looked at Clint. "What was your next move?"

"He was talking about going out to see Bennett," Inga said, "although I don't know how he planned to do that. He's in no condition to ride."

"Not a problem," Bat Masterson said. "I'll go and see him. Clint can stay here."

"I like that idea," Clint said. "It'll show Bennett what he's up against."

Bat stood up.

"Tell me something," he said to Clint. "What do you want the final outcome of this to be? Do you just want to get out?"

"If that was all I wanted, I could have sneaked out last night," Clint said. "I want someone to pay for every bullet I took."

"All the men who pulled the trigger are apparently dead," Bat said.

"That's okay," Clint said, "the man who paid them is still around."

"And so are the men who conceived the whole idea," Inga said.

"Well," Bat said, "while I'm gone, maybe you can decide how many of them you actually want dead."

"I'll give it some thought."

As Masterson walked to the door, Clint said, "Bat?"

"Yep?"

"Thanks."

"You'd do it for me," Bat said, and left.

"Is he really Bat Masterson?" Inga asked.

"Yes."

"And he's really your friend?"

"Maybe the best one I've got."

"What about the man we sent the telegram to?" she asked. "Hartman?"

"Rick Hartman," Clint said.

"Why didn't he come?"

"Rick doesn't leave Labyrinth much anymore," Clint said, "and he doesn't use a gun very much. No, I think we got the better part of the deal with Bat coming instead of Rick."

"So you think that the two of you can just kill everyone?"

Clint laughed and said, "Bat Masterson wouldn't agree to that even if I asked, Inga."

"But he said—"

"Bat kids," Clint said, "a lot."

"Oh."

"He just wants me to make up my mind what I want to do."

"And what is that?"

He thought a moment, then said, "I want to make a bunch of people sorry they ever heard of me. I think that would do it."

As Bat left Inga's shop, he took a glance out of the corner of his eye at the man across the street. He was in the doorway of the hardware store, which was open for business. He suddenly had an idea and started across, heading directly for the store.

As he approached, he could see the in the man's eyes that he wasn't sure what to do. After all, the store was open and Bat could simply be going inside to make some purchases.

So, as Bat approached, the man stepped to the side to let him by. Bat reached him, started to step past him, and then suddenly crowded him against the wall.

"Hey—" the man said.

Bat plucked the man's gun from his holster and said, "Quiet, friend. Don't talk unless I ask you a question."

"What the—"

Bat struck the man on the bridge of his nose with his own gun.

"Ow!" Instantly, a blossom of red appeared, and the man grabbed his nose.

"I said don't talk. Understand?"

The man stared at Masterson over his clasped hands and nodded.

"What's your name?"

The man stared.

"You can answer."

"Gunther."

"Who are you working for, Gunther? You can answer."

"Brian Bennett."

"Bennett himself?"

"No," Gunther said.

"Then who?"

"Dave Manners, the foreman."

"What are you supposed to do?"

"Just watch."

Bat eyed the man critically.

"You've been in prison, haven't you?"

"Yeah."

"How did you get to work for Bennett?"

"Dave—the foreman—I was in prison with him."

"What were you in for?"

"Robbery."

"And this Dave?"

"He killed his woman and a man he caught her with."

"How'd he kill her?"

"He broke her neck."

Clint had told Bat about Gloria Bennett and her broken neck.

"Okay, let's go."

"Where?"

Bat emptied the shells out of the man's gun and slid it back into his holster.

"We're gonna go see your boss."

FORTY-TWO

"Where do you think you're going?" Inga asked as Clint stood up and grabbed his gun belt.

"I'm not going to let Bat do all the work, since he just got here. I'm going over to talk to Mike Casey."

"And say what?"

"I'm going to give him a chance to give Bennett up as the man who paid to have me killed," Clint said, "and had his wife killed. If Casey testifies, I can have Bennett put away."

"And what about Mike? And the doctor?"

"I don't know," Clint said. "I guess I'll just have to see what the law wants to do with them. I'm sure Casey will have to turn in his badge."

"And the doctor? He saved your life."

"And he was in on the plot to take it," Clint said. "I think he's just going to have to play the hand that's dealt to him."

"And this will be enough for you?" she asked. "To have Bennett in jail? To have Mike Casey lose his job?"

"Well, Casey'll do more than lose his job."

"What do you mean?"

"He also moved Gloria Bennett's body and buried it. I'm no lawyer, but that's got to be against the law."

163

"What about the man who actually killed Gloria?"

Clint nodded and said, "I'll want him, too. But there's something I need to know from you."

"What's that?"

"If this whole town knew about this plot to kill me and went along with it," Clint asked, "who do I have to worry about taking a shot at me when I show up on the street?"

"No one," she said. "That was all supposed to be paid for by Bennett. Professional gunmen were supposed to be called in. I don't think any of these people would do anything."

"It would have been nice if you'd told me *that* sooner."

She smiled and said, "You never asked."

When Clint got downstairs to the front door, he saw Bat marching the man out of the hardware store doorway. He smiled. His friend couldn't resist grandstanding and was going to bring Brian Bennett his own man. Bat always did have style.

Clint left the shop and started toward the sheriff's office.

Masterson walked Gunther to the livery to get both his own horse and Gunther's.

"Lead the way, Gunther," he said, "and don't give me a reason to put a bullet in you. I only want to talk to your boss."

"Manners?"

"No, the big boss. Mr. Bennett."

"I don't know if he's gonna like that."

"Tell you what?" Bat said. "When I see him I'll ask him, and I'll let you know what he says."

Clint entered the sheriff's office without knocking. Somehow it didn't occur to him that Mike Casey wouldn't be there. Casey was sitting behind his desk.

"Adams," Casey said. "I didn't expect you so soon. In fact, I didn't expect to see you here."

"I'm wrapped up pretty tightly again, Sheriff. I think I'll live."

"Have you made up your mind?"

"Well," Clint said, "there are some things I'd like to talk to you about before I make my final decision."

"And what would those be?"

"Let me sit down," Clint said. "This may take a while."

FORTY-THREE

When Bat Masterson arrived at the Bennett ranch with Gunther, he let the other man do the talking. As it happened, they were braced by the foreman, Dave Manners.

"Gunther. What are you doing back? Who's this?"

"This fella wants to see Mr. Bennett, Boss."

"You had a job to do in Black Rock, Gunther," Manners said. "Who told you that you could bring a stranger back here."

"I really didn't have much choice, Boss."

Manners looked at Bat.

"Who are you, Mister?"

"I'll introduce myself to your boss, Brian Bennett."

"Mr. Bennett's a real busy man," Manners said. "Maybe I should just let you talk to Earl."

Clint had explained Earl to Bat.

"My understanding is that Earl doesn't talk much," Bat said. "Why don't I wait here with your man while you talk to your boss? Tell him this is about killing Clint Adams just to put a town on the map."

"I don't think he'll like—"

"Tell him it's about his dead wife."

Manners frowned.

"Mrs. Bennett is dead?"

"You ought to know," Bat said. "You killed her."

Manners couldn't hide the look on his face, and then he tossed a furious one at Gunther.

"Boss, I didn't tell him. Hell, I didn't know she was dead!"

Manners realized Gunther was right. He didn't know the woman was dead, so how could he have known that he'd killed her? But how did this man know?"

"Just go tell your boss what I said," Bat told him. "Let him decide what he wants to do."

Manners thought that over for a minute and then said, "Wait here," and went up to the house. It spoke volumes about his position that he had to knock on the door and speak to a servant before he could enter. Hell, he could kill his employer's wife but couldn't enter his house without permission.

They waited like that, both still mounted, for about ten minutes. When the door to the house opened this time, Manners stepped out with a bigger man behind him. Bat knew this had to be Earl.

"Follow Earl," Manners said. "He'll take you to the boss."

"Fine," Bat said and dismounted. He handed the reins of his horse to Manners, who took them before he realized what he was doing.

As he mounted the steps, he heard Manners and Gunther getting into it, and Gunther said something about his gun not being loaded.

"Lead the way, handsome," Bat said. Earl turned and walked away without bothering to see if Bat was following him.

He led the way to Bennett's office, where the man was waiting behind his desk. Just moments before, he had checked the gun in the top drawer of his desk—the one he'd used to kill Ed Cahill—to make sure that it was loaded.

Bat thought that Bennett and Earl made a very odd

couple. Both ugly, one small, and the other larger than life.

"What's this about my wife being dead? Who are you, Sir?"

"My name is Bat Masterson," Bat said. "I'm a friend of Clint Adams's. A good friend of his."

"I've heard of you," Bennett said, tossing a quick look at Earl.

"If he goes for that gun under his arm, or goes for *me*, he'll be dead before he knows it—and you'll be next."

Bennett took a moment to digest that and then tossed another look at Earl. The two men seemed to be able to communicate without speaking.

"I know who you are," Bennett said, again, "but I don't know why you're here, why you're threatening me and my employee, and what you're talking about. What's this about Gloria being—"

"Mr. Bennett," Bat said, "we're not going to get anywhere if you're going to try to play me for a fool. None of this has fooled Clint Adams one bit. He knows you paid to have him killed. He knows you had your foreman kill your wife and plant her body in the sheriff's house. I know all this because he told me. I'm here to tell you that no one is playing your game anymore. Clint is on his feet, his gun is strapped on, and he's going to come for you."

"Here?" Bennett almost squeaked.

"Definitely."

"But I have men," Bennett said, "I have Earl."

"None of this will help you," Bat said. "See, Clint has help, too. He's got me, and he's got the sheriff."

"The sheriff?"

"I understand the sheriff is a pretty good hand with a gun. The three of us can work our way through your defenses, I think. Hell, look at how easily I got in here."

"What makes you think it would be as easy for you to get back out?" Bennett asked.

"I only see you and Earl here, sir," Bat said. "I don't doubt you've got a gun in that top drawer, the way you're looking at it. Earl might be good with that shoulder rig, but he'll never get the gun out in time to beat me—and you'll never get yours out of your drawer. But, see, there's no reason for us to mess up your office. I'm just here to deliver a message."

"That Clint Adams is coming to kill me?"

"He intends to come and kill you," Bat said, "but he's not dead-set on it—if you know what I mean."

Bennett frowned and looked at Earl. The big man had not taken his eyes off of Bat Masterson since they entered the office together.

"I don't understand," Bennett said. "What do you mean he's not dead-set on it?"

"Let me explain. . . ."

FORTY-FOUR

"You're crazy," Casey said.

"Why?"

"I'm not gonna give myself up," the sheriff said. "I'll give you Bennett, sure. I'll say he killed his wife."

"You can't prove that," Clint said. "You didn't see him."

"I'll say he hired men to kill you."

"If you give yourself up," Clint said, "your testimony will stand up better."

"Not a chance."

"Then tell me why I should back you against Bennett?"

"I did tell you," Casey said. "You need me to stay alive as badly as I need you."

"You have plenty of men in town."

Casey made a rude noise with his mouth. "These sheep? They only went along with the plan because they wouldn't have to do anything."

"So I never really had to worry about going against a whole town," Clint said. "I only had to worry about you."

"And Bennett and his men."

"So once we got rid of Bennett, I'd have to go back to worrying about you again?"

"No," Casey said, "once we get rid of him, you and I are quits. We wouldn't need each other anymore."

"And you'd get away with plotting my murder," Clint said. "Is that it?"

"You're alive," Casey said. "That should count for something."

"What about the doctor?" Clint asked. "Would he testify?"

"Testify, yes," Casey said, "but he wouldn't give himself up any more than I would."

"Would he give Bennett up?"

"In a second."

"And would he give you up?"

"Not a chance."

"You're sure of that?"

"Dead sure."

"Maybe I should go and talk to him." Clint stood up.

"I'll go with you," Casey said, starting to rise.

"No, I think I should talk to him alone."

"I can't let you do that, Adams," the sheriff said.

"Then you don't trust him?"

"Maybe it's you I don't trust."

"How could you not trust me and want me to watch your back?"

"I'm getting the feeling that's not gonna happen."

"I think you're right," Clint said. "In fact, I've got somebody who will watch my back. He's out talking to Bennett right now."

"Who? Who's gonna back you?"

"A friend of mine who rode into town today," Clint said. "His name is Bat Masterson."

Casey froze for a moment.

"Bat Masterson is in town?"

"Well, not exactly in town," Clint said. "He's out talking to Brian Bennett at the moment."

"It was that telegraph message Inga sent, wasn't it?" Casey asked. "It made no sense to me, but it must have been some kind of code."

"What does it matter?" Clint asked. His breathing was becoming labored because the bandages were so tight, but he thought he was successfully hiding the fact. "All that matters is that he's here."

"Why's he talking to Bennett?"

"To see if he'll give you up."

"I see," Casey said. "You want us to testify against each other that we hatched a plot to kill you."

"That would be very helpful."

Casey sat back in his chair and smiled.

"You know," he said, "under normal circumstances, I think I could take you."

"Is that a fact?"

"Yep," Casey said. "I'm younger, and faster—but now that you're injured, I know I can."

"I see," Clint said. "You wouldn't kill me while I was in bed, but now you want me out in the street? Is that it? That will still accomplish your goal for this town. And it would do a lot for your reputation, as well."

"I'm not looking for a reputation," Casey said. "I'm just not gonna turn myself in. If you insist on that . . ."

"And I do."

". . . then I have only one other option."

"Kill me?"

"It's my guess that if Bat Masterson went out to see Bennett alone," Casey said, "he's already dead. Earl probably took care of him. Without you around, maybe Bennett and I can come to an understanding."

"Does this mean you don't want me to watch your back anymore?" Clint asked.

"I think you're gonna have to go back to watching your own, Adams," Casey said.

"So you'll make up with Bennett and let him get away with having his wife killed and trying to blame you?"

"We'll come to an understanding," Casey said. "We have before."

"I think you have a problem, Sheriff."

"And what's that?"

"I think you're underestimating Bat Masterson and me," Clint said, "and overestimating yourself."

Casey stared at Clint. The man wasn't standing properly. He was stiff and probably in pain, but he was on his feet and dressed. Out on the street he'd look normal.

The lawman didn't think he had a choice anymore. He'd have to alter his plan. If he took care of Adams first, he could concentrate on Bennett later. Right now, his primary problem was Clint Adams.

"We can go out into the street, Adams," Casey said. "If you outdraw me, you can leave this town with no problems."

"Well, that makes us even, then," Clint said.

"How so?"

"If I kill you," Clint said, "all your problems will be solved . . . permanently."

FORTY-FIVE

Bat sensed that something was happening in the room. He'd pushed, expecting them to back up, and instead they were going to push back.

"Think about it, Earl," he said. "Is what Bennett is paying you worth dying for?"

"There's more than money at stake here, Masterson," Bennett said.

"Like what?"

"Self-respect."

"His or yours?"

"Both," Bennett said. "You see, Earl and I have a lot in common. We've formed a bond. He is loyal to me."

"I wonder how loyal you are to him?"

"Meaning what?"

"Meaning if Earl and I go against each other?"

"What are you proposing?"

"Earl and me, winner take all," Bat said. "If he kills me, then you've won."

"And if you kill him?"

"Adams and I get to leave town, and you testify against the sheriff."

"And what about me?"

"You go free."

Bennett cocked his head, seeming to actually consider the proposition.

"Why would you make such an offer?"

"Maybe I don't think I can take the both of you."

"I've never heard anything about you lacking confidence, Masterson," Bennett said.

"Make your choice, Bennett. Either go for that gun in your desk, or let Earl take me alone."

"You'd never get out of here alive," Bennett said. "My men are all outside."

Bat smiled.

"Do you really think they'd go up against me once the man who pays them is dead?"

Bennett had to think for a minute.

"You're doing this for Adams? Risking your own life?"

"We have a bond, Bennett," Bat said. "It's called friendship. Come on. Make the call."

Bennett looked at Bat, then Earl, and then at Bat again.

Clint left the sheriff's office and walked back to Inga's shop. He did not go in, however. He had been willing himself not to break out into a sweat while in Casey's presence, but now the sweats came with a vengeance. He decided that while he was up, he'd better stay up.

Inga was waiting for him at the door and rushed to his side.

"My God, you're gray—and wet. Come back to bed."

"I can't," he said. "I pushed Casey, and he pushed back. It's going to end today."

"What? You're going to kill him?"

"Or him, me," Clint said. "If he kills me, your town may grow after all."

"Clint, you can't do this. You're in no shape."

"I'm a little sweaty, that's all," he said, trying to dry the palm of his gun hand on his thigh. He didn't want to tell her that his knees were also weak and his head was pounding.

"Go inside, Inga," Clint said. "This has to happen."

"And after you kill him? Then what? Is the doctor next?"

He waved her away. In his head he wondered if the sheriff was right. Had Bat walked into a hornet's nest and gotten himself killed? No, Bat could handle himself.

He was certainly in better shape for this kind of nonsense then he was right now.

"Look at him, Earl," Bat said. "He's going to let you go against me one on one."

Bennett had pushed his chair back from his desk, away from the drawer with the gun in it.

Bat turned to face Earl, but the big man wasn't looking at him. He was looking at Bennett.

"You son of a bitch," Earl said.

Bennett knew what was going to happen. He lunged for his desk drawer desperately, because he knew he'd pushed Earl's loyalty too far. He never got the drawer open. Earl came out with his gun, a remarkably quick move for a big man drawing from a shoulder rig. The first bullet struck Bennett in the chest, the second in the throat, and the third in the forehead.

Then, to Bat's not-total-surprise, Earl turned on him. Bat drew, because he'd half expected this from the big man. After all, the man he'd formed his bond with was dead.

Bat had no time to speak. He shot Earl three times in the chest, because he doubted one or two shots would stop the man. The three bullets stopped him, all right, but they didn't put him down. The gun was still in his hand, and Bat had no choice. His next shot was a head shot, and Earl hit the floor.

Bat ejected the spent shells from his gun and quickly recovered. Bennett had been right about one thing. He had a lot of men outside, like Dave Manners and Gunther. What remained to be seen was whether or not Bat was right. Once they knew their boss was dead, would they let him pass?

FORTY-SIX

"Oh God . . ." Inga said. "There he is. What fools men are!"

"Go inside, Inga," Clint said. "Don't watch."

"What's the difference?" she asked. "One man who I care about—or cared about—is going to die, whether I watch or not."

As Sheriff Casey stepped into the street, Clint looked at the buildings surrounding them. People were at the windows because this was what they had been waiting for. They hadn't gotten to watch anything when the five men kicked in Inga's door and started firing at Clint. This was the way a man who lived by the gun was supposed to die—on the street, facing another man with a gun.

Clint had doubts for the first time in years. He didn't know how fast Casey was, but he had killed five men recently. The thing that concerned him most, however, was his physical condition. His hand was still sweating. Would he be able to grip the gun? Would his legs hold him? Would the headache he was suffering become a blinding headache? Or would the sweat pouring from his brown hair simply run into his eyes, blinding him at

179

the wrong moment? Was he taped so tightly it would inhibit his ability with a gun?

Clint stepped into the street, because this was the only way to find out the answers. He walked toward the sheriff, who had already stopped. It was up to Clint then, to choose the distance.

When he kept walking and it became clear to Casey that he was going to come even closer, the lawman shouted, "That's far enough, Adams. Don't try to intimidate me."

"I'm the one intimidated, Sheriff."

"Is that a fact?"

"I've never shot a man wearing a badge."

"You mean if I kept it on you won't fire?"

"No, I'll fire, but I'll hate myself tomorrow."

"Well, I'll save you from that," Casey said. He reached up with his left hand, unpinned the badge from his shirt, and tossed it into the dirt. At the same moment, he went for his gun with his right hand, looking for any edge he could get.

Clint expected something like this and was ready for it. He drew his gun, his palm wet and tacky on the handle of his revolver. He closed his hand around it and drew it and was satisfied to find that it did not slip from his grip.

He fired twice, and his legs almost gave out. He watched as two small eruptions of red appeared on Mike Casey's chest—one right where the badge would have been had he kept it on.

Clint certainly would have hated himself in the morning if he'd fired right through that tin star.

The sheriff stood there for a moment, gun still in his holster, then wavered and fell onto his face in the dirt. Clint heard something behind him, turned, and saw Bat Masterson behind him.

"Nice move," Bat said.

•   •   •

It was another week before Clint felt well enough to leave Black Rock on a horse. Bennett was dead, as was Earl and the sheriff. The doctor had left town the day after Clint shot Casey. He was probably still running.

The people of Black Rock decided their town was just fine the size that it was. Inga was trying to sell her store so she could leave.

Bat explained to Clint that after he killed Bennett, his ranch hands decided not to try him, especially not for free. No one knew what was going to happen to Bennett's ranch now that he and his wife were dead. (She'd been dug up and buried properly.) All anyone knew was that no one was out there now, except maybe Cyrus, the black servant. Dave Manners and his friends had left, and the other hands soon followed.

If it was possible, Black Rock was back to normal for the first time since someone—Doc Milburn, Sheriff Casey, maybe even Inga, for all he knew—first raised the possibility of putting themselves on the map by killing the Gunsmith.

Clint rode Duke up to the front of the apothecary shop, which was open for business again. Inga came out and looked up at him. They had not really touched since the day he killed Casey—not in any sexual way. She continued to care for him, especially in the absence of the doctor, but that was all. Watching him kill Mike Casey had done something to her conception of him. That was okay. He'd seen it happen before.

He looked down at her from high atop Duke's back, where he hadn't been for some time. He felt very comfortable being back in the saddle.

"You should rest some more," she said.

"Time to go," he said.

"I know."

"I wish you luck," he said, "wherever you end up."

She hesitated, then said, "I'm . . . sorry, Clint."

"Nothing to be sorry for, Inga," he said. "Maybe you're the only person in this town who can say that."

He turned and rode off, and she was the only person who really knew how wrong she was.

Her and her big ideas.

Watch for

THE CLEVELAND CONNECTION

218th novel in the exciting GUNSMITH series
from Jove

Coming in February!

J. R. ROBERTS
THE GUNSMITH

Prices slightly higher in Canada

Payable in U.S. funds only. No cash/COD accepted. Postage & handling: U.S./CAN. $2.75 for one book, $1.00 for each additional, not to exceed $6.75; Int'l $5.00 for one book, $1.00 each additional. We accept Visa, Amex, MC ($10.00 min.), checks ($15.00 fee for returned checks) and money orders. Call 800-788-6262 or 201-933-9292, fax 201-896-8569; refer to ad # 206 (10/99)

Penguin Putnam Inc. P.O. Box 12289, Dept. B Newark, NJ 07101-5289 Please allow 4-6 weeks for delivery. Foreign and Canadian delivery 6-8 weeks.	Bill my: ❑ Visa ❑ MasterCard ❑ Amex _____(expires) Card# _____ Signature _____

Bill to:

Name _____

Address _____ City _____

State/ZIP _____ Daytime Phone # _____

Ship to:

Name _____ Book Total $ _____

Address _____ Applicable Sales Tax $ _____

City _____ Postage & Handling $ _____

State/ZIP _____ Total Amount Due $ _____

This offer subject to change without notice.

JAKE LOGAN
TODAY'S HOTTEST ACTION WESTERN!

LONGARM

Explore the exciting Old West with one of the men who made it wild!